REAL

SHAREEKA ELLIOTT

DYNAMIC IMAGE PUBLICATIONS

REAL
By SHAREEKA ELLIOTT

Published by Dynamic Image Publications LLC
PO Box 3051
Alton, IL 62002
dipublications.com

Cover Image by: Brion & Rachel Whigham
Cover by: Christian Cashelle & Jasmine Clayborn of Dynamic Image

ISBN-13: 979-8-9852060-5-0

Library of Congress Control Number: 2026933152

First Edition: March 2026

Manufactured in the United States of America

Other titles by Shareeka Elliott

Green

REAL

Chapter One

Kiara David

Midnight marked my 32nd birthday and I thought I would've been more excited. The spot next to me on our king-sized bed was as empty as I felt. My bed was cold. My body felt the same even as I snuggled under an all-weather down comforter with my feet rubbing together. The ever present ache I'd grown used to having was my only company as I tried to ignore the fact that I had no clue where my man was.

Multiple birthday wishes started climbing in, temporarily pulling me away from the pain I was experiencing. There was one in particular I lingered on. The automatic smile that pulled on my face couldn't be denied as a one Johnathan Barnes' message pushed through.

"You's an ole lady now. I bought you a wheelchair so you can at least get around a lil' bit. All jokes aside, you know I had to be first. Happy birthday, beautiful. Let me know if you busy later."

I thanked him, making sure a middle finger emoji was present in the mix. I thought of my best friend in the world and bit my lip, wondering why I still called him such.

Johnathan was a huge part of my life ever since I met him and his band of childhood friends in Georgia. Our friendship started innocently enough. I was the only girl for miles into the same weird crap the guys were into, genuinely. Some girls wanted their attention and so suddenly they were into Pokémon, Digimon, Power Rangers, and the list went on. I wanted to learn how to fight, rough and tumble with the best of them, and my band of friends were the best of them.

Of course, age set in and maturity caused me to distance myself from them and make girlfriends who would help me tap into my femininity. That's where Shaunte Aldana came in around junior high school. I'd still been rough around the edges, but I was slowly understanding the power of lip gloss and how taking the time to wrap my hair at night gave the best results for the next morning. My mother was grateful. Before Shaunte's influence, I cared nothing about looking the part past, not smelling like a garbage disposal.

I still wasn't sure of when my love for Johnathan came in. Even lying awake at night, with no clue where my long-term boyfriend was at or who he was entertaining, I wondered at the moment my feelings had turned from familial to lustful.

And boy, did I lust.

He was a bronze Adonis. I was already a shorter woman but standing next to Johnathan further drove the point home that I was only 5 '4 to this 6' 2. There was a time when I was convinced that his body was crafted with iron and every muscle, every singular sinew that fastened him together was masterfully put together by God and nobody else. That was around the time I saw Johnathan as a man and not just my best friend, amongst the friends that I had. I was unsure if separation and my personal journey into becoming a woman had sparked the attraction or if our closeness in general was a precursor. Some people find their soulmates early in life and don't realize it.

Still, I was unsure of his feelings toward me. While I knew I loved him, I was also in my own situation and had been since senior year of high school. Julien had been the one to pursue me and for a while I'd been in love with him. His persistence had won me over and for a time romance reigned supreme in our relationship. It had until somewhere along the line, everything became more about him than about us.

He built a career in finance, and I built mine in tech as a software engineer. I made pretty good money but Julien had always made more. His former career in the NFL hadn't panned out and I think every day he lived in that regret and in turn, I had a great deal of emotional labor to contend with. It had paid off once he made his pivot into finance. Thankfully, he pursued the major while on scholarship with Morehouse.

The more Julien progressed in his career however, the less I saw him. After many days of him being a piteous shell of a man, the years after he got back on his feet were worse. It was like I'd never been there for him. I was fairly certain his new assistant was taking up most of his time these days, yet I had no concrete proof. The thought that she was getting the better part of him lent itself to the ache in my heart. I had to breathe in slowly and deeply to fight the undertows of sadness that threatened to take me under.

Aimlessly scrolling through my phone, thoughts of my best friend filled me with warmth. Most of the people in my life remembered my birthday, but Johnathan always remembered to hit me up at midnight to celebrate me.

I went to my contacts, into my favorites, and my finger hovered over my man's name. I wasn't sure whether it made sense to contact him. I was feeling empty and although I knew Julien wasn't the man that I wanted to lie next to, or even talk to at this time of night, he was still my man. I was saddened that he wasn't bringing in my birthday with sex or hell, even a gift. No flowers littered my living room. I've told him a thousand times I love flowers. Sneakers that I mentioned wanting weren't even being delivered in any Amazon trucks. I'm not materialistic, I just thought the man that claimed to love me all these years would at least listen to me. These days, I was pretty sure he was just waiting for the moment I decided to leave.

My finger also hovered over Johnathan's name. I already knew his tenor would lull me to sleep. He hadn't always had the smoothest verbiage in the world to turn me on but still, he did. Stretching as far back into my memory as I could, he always had. It just never manifested into the grown feelings until I started burgeoning. Johnathan was a straight-shooter and sometimes romance and finery was lost on him. Still, I often wondered at the possibility of his brand of romance. I just knew I would thrive in it. Mostly because his friendship was healing to me.

It always has been.

I was embarrassed because I knew by the end of today, I'd be calling Johnathan with sadness. I knew my man wasn't going to turn up until my birthday was past tense, apologizing for his absence and tossing a few dollars my way. I hated how he always threw money at a problem. I told him time and again that money didn't turn me on. I didn't like how he weaponized it, the more his income bracket increased.

I was often lonely in the past two years. We always had a rocky relationship but somehow, we always came back to each other and made things work. There were times he would come back and there were times I would. More often than not, however, things were his fault. Julien was often selfish, and I'd take his nonsense until I couldn't. Other times, my insecurity pushed him away. Other moments, I had to admit to myself, it didn't look good when Johnathan came to my rescue.

I often used him as my sounding board and Johnathan listened, offering solutions whether he wanted to or not. I would cry and curse my boyfriend's name just to go back. Most people respected it but there were those who hated that I stayed with Julien when Johnathan so "obviously" loved me.

Still, my best friend had his own fans, and he didn't turn them down. There had been moments when I thought things would turn but...back in college, Johnathan was popular. He and his boys were frat boys. They turned up at parties and I saw first-hand how women went out of their way for him. Could I blame him?

He was at the prime of his life and I'd be selfish to expect loyalty of that standard when I was still with Julien.

The way I saw it, he had to say something in order for something to happen. I could assume his feelings all I wanted to, but I'd look stupid if he did nothing about it.

I sighed, deciding to open the Photos app and look through pictures of us. I wanted to text Johnathan and bother him with some of the goofier pictures I'd taken of him but went against the feeling. I melted at our group photos with friends. I sighed at pictures we'd taken together. I wondered if I'd see steamier pictures of us on my phone during my lifetime. My heart began to ache as my desire started to overwhelm me. I closed out the app, groaning as the dull ache started to burn in my heart.

I tossed my phone aside as I stared at the empty space in my bed once more, laughing bitterly at myself for being such a joke before my tiredness overtook my body.

Johnathan Barnes

I winced as I considered how much money I'd have to hand over in a few hours' time. Still, walking through the hotel space where Kiara's birthday party was being decorated showed me that Shaunte Aldana's efforts were worth every penny. I was pleased with all I was seeing, and it wasn't even totally finished yet.

"Shaunte, you did your thing," I confessed, taking everything in. "I didn't know you were on this level."

My friend beamed, her smile bright enough to light up any room. It was super apparent what made Micah claim her years ago. Still, in my mind she was no contest to the little woman who I knew to be home on her big day, saddened because her actual man was slacking and had been for a long time.

Somewhere in between sophomore year and junior year of high school, I'd fallen for Kiara David. Shaunte thought it'd be cute to put my best friend in something other than baggy jeans and oversized t-shirts. The discovery of what had been hiding still left me on semi-hard most days. Her smooth, pretty caramel skin glowed. Kiara was what we liked to call slim-thick. From head to toe she was balanced perfectly. Her breasts were just big enough. Her backside was just big enough. Her waist was the perfect hourglass and most nights I could picture my hands making their home there while I...you get the picture.

"You damn right I am," Shaunte said. "Still, some of this was thrown in for free as you can imagine. Key is my girl and now that you're making a move, I had to be a part of the antics. It's past time for Julien to go!"

The laughter came from the pit of my stomach at her candidness. I wasn't going to deny that this party was mostly my way of shooting my shot. Still, Kiara was extraordinary to me. She wasn't like anybody else so I wouldn't treat her as such. Besides, at the end of the day she was still my best friend. I just wanted her to see her value. Most men got away with murder because women didn't understand their worth.

Kiara was more than worthy to me, and I wanted her to see it, too. She was even worth more than this party I was throwing in her honor.

"I'm glad you're on my team, Shaun."

"I am, now. I wanted to slap the shit out of you for years. You let this go on for too long," she giggled. "But nah, you my boy. She's my girl. I got y'all."

Bust three times throw up the peace sign she sleep, then my dick sleep and I ain't got to call her for weeks...

Both of us turned to Xander, who was overseeing the sound check on the stage. He pulled out his phone and muted the ringtone that caused me to laugh. Ever since we heard Nas' and his homeboy's singular hit, it became one of Xander's favorite songs. It always amused me, but Shaunte not so much.

"His nasty ass..." she mumbled. "Would it kill him to put that shit on mute?"

I didn't make a comment, just threw my hands up, turning my attention back on the rest of the details of the decorative elements Shaunte had going on.

Still, I thought about the food. I thought about the rental price. I thought about the dress I paid for that I was hoping to see on the floor by the time the night was over. The hotel room with balcony space and a king-sized bed that I was ready to use every square inch to wear her out on. It was a long time coming. I ached to call her again and see where her head was at but I refrained. I knew I couldn't hear her voice be extra sad or else I was going to confess like the weenie I was for her.

My friends and I came together in a circle after most of the preparations were over and done with.

Bust three times...

Bust three times...

Bust three times...

"Yo! Turn your phone off! Nobody wants to keep hearing that shit over and over."

Shaunte's voice cracked through the air like lightning, forcing Xander to cackle at her expense. The tiredness in Micah's face already told the story of the way Xander and Shaunte probably already argued more times than we knew about before this moment. They were prone to argue like siblings.

"Shaunte′...not today." Micah said, his voice weary. "Y'all two fight it out another day but not today."

Xander chuckled, pulling his phone out of his pocket and muting it.

"Nah, she got it. I'll put it on mute."

I was grateful, mostly because Xander's phone would ring about twenty more times before we all went our separate ways, and it was for the best. I was getting tired of hearing it myself, but certain things hit differently when a woman said it.

"You don't get a break though? Your dick ain't tired?"

I shook my head at the too-direct question as Xander sucked his teeth.

"Never," he said. "Bitches love me and I love the bitches!"

Xander pulled out his phone and moments later to my dismay, the beat drop to Oochie Wally sounded over the speakers the team just set up. Helpless laughter left me as Shaunte´ glared at Xander, full annoyance spilling over. Xander shoulder bounced to the beat and Micah joined in, doing a shoulder bounce that caused his woman to lightly shove at him. A few more moments after, Xander cut the music with laughter still present on his face.

"Sound system is solid," he reported, causing Shaunte´ to roll her eyes.

"Listen. I have about fifteen thousand more things to do before this party and being here slowed me down. If you weren't my man's boy, you'd be paying extra for this shit."

As it were I planned to anyway, but I understood the sentiment. It caused me to smile sideways and side hug her.

"I got love for you, Tay."

My smile forced her to smile.

"Anyway, everything is on schedule to be finished well before the party," she said. "All I need is for you to make sure you procure payment to me before the end of the night-tomorrow the latest-and I'll have your receipt in the next two to three business days."

I nodded. "Cool. Lovely doing business with you. Now that that's out of the way, who's going to pick up Kiara for me?"

"We can't or else you won't have a surprise. Uriel can't because...he's a bitch made nigga and Xander can't because if he shows up with Kiara all the bitches won't want to talk to him," Micah said, forcing laughter out of me.

"Actually, I thought you were the best choice, Xander." His face twisted up, asking what made me think that. "Well, you're good at making Kiara laugh and if this nigga screws up her birthday as usual then I know she'll be sad by the time she calls me about it."

Xander laughed, no doubt amused by my confidence of how the situation was already playing out. Honestly, it was sad, but it was the truth of the situation. Julien had grown lazy, and Kiara didn't put any fear in his heart to move differently. I was getting ready to rock his world because I'd grown tired of waiting on the sidelines while he left her at home to be lonely. It was time to cure that and be done with him.

Kiara David belonged to me, and it was high time I started acting like it.

Chapter Two

Kiara David

"I hate this nigga to death."

I was again lamenting to Johnathan about Julien. More than twelve hours later, there'd been not one call. There'd been not one text. I went through a workday just to keep myself occupied. I went through the motions after work and decided to have a self-care day. It was about six o'clock when I finally let the sadness take over because my boyfriend decided to blatantly forget my birthday again. At this point it was embarrassing to even complain to my friend, but he was there.

"What happened?"

Johnathan's voice soothed me while I complained. I'd been pacing back and forth in our living room, my bare feet creating a shallow path on cream carpeted floors. I glanced over at our cream cloud couch, aching to sit down but anxiety pushed me to continue blazing the same insane path.

It was ironic that every inch of my house was made for comfort but yet there was none to be found in the moment I was having.

"He didn't call at all today, Johnny. Didn't even come home from last night. Like what the fuck?! I'm not even worth a Happy Birthday?!"

"We both know you're worth more than that. Been with him too long for him to forget."

Tears were in my throat when I said, "Man, fuck him. I'm through with him, I promise!"

Of course, I'd said the same thing time and again. Each time, Johnny never had feedback for me. I realized after some time I waited for him to say something but each and every time he said nothing.

"What you doing, though? I'll get Xander to pick you up and we'll get together and do a lil' somethin'."

"All of us? Make sure Shaun is there and Lashawn, too. I can't be sitting up under y'all niggas all night."

I heard the smirk in his voice. "I got you, although I think I'm not a bad nigga to be up under."

I felt my face warm at the thought that he was the one I wanted to be up under all night. Still, if it was a group assignment, then I had to make do with what I got.

"I'm sure you're not, Johnny. Still."

"Aight, so I'm gonna get ready and Xander gonna grab you. Cool?"

"Fuck it. Can't waste my whole birthday crying."

Johnathan chuckled. "Stop pouting. You'll be alright."

It was on that note that the call ended and I waited for the call from Xander. About twenty-five minutes later I got a text before the bell rang.

I walked up to the door, peeking through and questioning why Xander was standing outside holding a garment bag. I opened the door, asking him the same question. He smirked after he leaned in to give me a chaste kiss on the cheek.

"Happy Birthday, Key. This is from Johnny-Boy."

I snickered, knowing that Johnathan hated the name but Xander always insisted on calling him that.

"A dress?"

Confused, I took the dress from him and opened the garment bag. I pulled out a beautiful, royal blue bodycon dress. It was sexy yet not too provocative. The top of the dress criss crossed over the breast area while the rest of it would hug me tighter than a lover. I mentally ran through what shoes I had in my closet that would pair well with the dress. After that I remembered a jewelry set that I'd just purchased not long ago that would set the outfit off. As I put everything together in my mind I squealed, excitement suddenly taking over as I told Xander to give me a few minutes. That was before I doubled back and looked my friend in the eye.

"Johnny picked this out?"

Xander shook his head, "I don't know the details on that. Shaunte probably had something to do with it, but I know for certain John bought it."

I smirked, thinking that made sense. Still, I didn't even know what was going on.

"Where are we going?" I questioned. "This is giving planned out instead of on the fly."

"Sis, we all knew this nigga was going to drop the ball. So, hurry your ass up and get dressed so we can get right."

I giggled, saddened that my life had become that predictable as it stood with my boyfriend. Without any more questions, I ran upstairs, through my expansive master bedroom and into the equally impressive master bath. I custom designed the space myself and because the budget was there, I wanted to have a separate shower from a standing bathtub. Double sinks were a must for me since I shared the space with my boyfriend and I didn't want to share the small space that would be set apart for me.

I stepped past the glass door and closed it, taking my time to freshen up but kept my speed at a steady pace since I understood that I had a limited time to get ready.

Once I was all freshened up from the shower I walked into my neutral colored bedroom and sat at my vanity to finish up.

While I had, again, Johnathan's moves weighed on my mind. It seemed Johnathan was already a few steps ahead and I wondered exactly what was planned for the evening because this was a turn that my friend never took. The dress alone was enough to melt me as I slid it on and looked at myself in the mirror.

My hair had been wrapped so all there was to do was let down my lengths after I applied my makeup. I went for a quick, neutral look but made sure to smoke out my eyes just enough so that I came across sexy. I was tempted to FaceTime Shaunte because I knew my friend knew what was going on. I abandoned the idea, also knowing she wasn't going to tell me much.

Johnathan was on my mind front and center as I did another twirl. Suddenly, the urge to want to take this dress off for his viewing pleasure became overwhelming but I pumped the brakes on those thoughts. I had to feel out the temperature first before I embarrassed myself. He was still my best friend and probably just wanted me to have a good night. I had to admit to being blessed by every friend that I had and didn't want to ever take their friendship for granted.

I presented myself to Xander about forty minutes later and knew I'd put myself together well as my friend eyed me in appreciation.

"You came a long way, Key. Used to look like rough and tumble and now you got niggas wanting to rough and tumble your little ass."

I shoulder bumped my friend as he helped me out of the door with a chuckle.

"I have to grow up at some point, Xan," I said, giggling. "It just sucks to do it alone."

Xander edged a look at me and shrugged.

"We're born alone and then we die alone. But of course, Key, you have to take in stock how you feel about you and tell that nigga where to go. I don't know who told you to keep taking this nigga's bullshit, but you know you don't have to, right? I don't even have to tell you that you deserve better. Like sis, you have to know it."

"I know, bro," I sighed.. "I know."

"I hope you do. But just have fun tonight. We got you."

I smiled as my friend helped me into his car and we peeled off into the night. Excitement bubbled in my system as I wondered what was in store.

I bogged down Xander with questions-a-plenty but he didn't give me so much as a hint. Forcing me to sit in quiet anticipation I watched as my suburban Queens neighborhood eased into the unique ruggedness of

Brooklyn. After a time, the ruggedness changed over to the more refined, gentrified areas leading to downtown Brooklyn. Xander finally stopped in front of the new Hudson-Mason hotel. I'd grown even more excited, having heard they were the pinnacle of luxury and the new standard in New York City for luxe hotel stays.

Still, nothing I imagined prepared me for what was on the other side of Downtown, Brooklyn.

Johnathan Barnes

The Pigeon is about to enter the Hornet's nest.

I scoffed at the foolish text message that Xander sent but had to admit shock that he'd gotten Kiara to the spot on time. I'd been stressed in between getting ready, making it on time myself and wondering how Xander had the time to knock some chick down amid him doing what I asked of him. I told Micah that it was show time and then made my way to the DJ. Once I gave him the signal, he instructed the crowd to get quiet and the lights dimmed in the event space.

Before I was ready about five minutes later, Kiara made her appearance, and the crowd went wild. I knew the mixture of shock that she looked like a vision plus the excitement that she finally showed up was the cause of her eyes shining and tears falling. I looked into her eyes from my vantage point, realizing she was truly moved at the display, and I felt my heart ache at the realization that nobody ever thought to throw her a huge party, just because.

Of course, I had. I wanted my gesture to be grand because that's who she was to me. She was special and I felt that before she died, she needed to see how special she was, not only to me but to others. Sometimes in romantic situations when your partner failed to show you what you mean to them, you start to believe it and I felt it was on me to show her that she was worth so much more than what Julien showed her.

The dress I'd chosen fit her body like a glove, and I was envious of the material that hugged her the way I wanted to. I yearned to stamp myself all over her until she almost couldn't figure out where she ended and where I began. The golden accessories she wore elevated the dress. Her bob she wore was effortlessly sexy. I felt myself go rigid fully taking her in.

Xander walked in behind her, his eyes telling me that if Kiara had been anybody other than his long-time friend, he would've tried it. I felt my fists closing in, wanting to hurt him for even the mere thought but stopped. Xander was good at baiting me but also, he was a red-blooded male and I had to humble myself. Most of the men in attendance were taking in the birthday girl. All the women were as well.

It was her moment after all.

Shaunte stepped in, taking her by the hand and I knew my friend was trying to guide her to where me and the others sat in a VIP section. They'd been slowed down by well-wishers and other men who wanted to try their luck. I watched Kiara smile politely although the look on her face read confusion. She was still trying to piece everything together but was failing to.

"Man, if you're not her man by the end of tonight, I don't know what to tell you."

I looked up at Uriel as he sat next to me, a drink in his hand. We watched the twosome float around in bemusement. I realized Shaunte stopped trying to work against the crowd because they weren't letting up. I was only fine with it because I got to take in my love without having to rush. It was a blessing because I could admire the dress I'd chosen (with Shaunte's help). It was a curse because all I wanted to do was take it off her. I wasn't too sure of the chances of that happening.

I lightly punched my friend on the arm, even as I saw his girlfriend, Lashawn, smoothly dancing towards him. I grinned at her as she flashed a smile at me, and laughter left me as she motioned towards Kiara.

"That dress is gorgeous, John," she said. "Tell L to get me one."

"I don't know, baby," Uriel said. "John spent a fortune on that one."

Lashawn smirked and gave him a coquettish stare. "So you're not going to even try? I thought you loved me."

Uriel was a fool over Lashawn though. It didn't have to be said that if Lashawn truly wanted that dress, Uriel was going to buy it for her. The price alone made me feel embarrassed to buy it, but I knew Kiara would look beautiful in it.

"You know I do. That price was still crazy though."

Lashawn grinned. "So cheap. Come dance with me. Maybe I can get a drink out of you."

"Maybe you can get two."

Seeing where Uriel's mind was headed caused me to laugh as they took their exit. About ten minutes later, Shaunte and Kiara finally reached me. I stood as Shaunte removed the rope, allowing her to reach me. We locked eyes and I watched hers fill up all over again as realization hit.

"You did this, Johnny?"

I felt like a schoolboy readying to ask out my crush on a first date. Still, the feeling couldn't compare. I nodded, watching her smile widen and my heart palpitated. I hadn't seen her smile that wide in a long time. The knowledge of that made my heart ache, knowing how much she put into her relationship with Julien. I was essentially doing his job but he didn't have to worry any longer.

That burden no longer belonged to him.

"I can't believe it. This is so...it's just so much!"

I laughed. "The night didn't even start yet, Key."

Her watery giggles started to overflow once Micah appeared with her birthday sash. A white ribbon that read 'Birthday Girl' in blue cursive script was laid over her dress. Micah pulled her in for a hug afterward.

"Happy Birthday, sis. Stop all this crying though! I thought we were Gs!"

Kiara's eyes were on me as she ignored Micah's quip and she wiped her eyes again, words escaping her. I opened my arms, and she didn't hesitate to walk into them, her arms reaching up to close around my neck. My own closed around her waist and I rocked her back and forth. We were close with no polite space between us and I took in the scent mix of amber, jasmine and vanilla. I felt myself start to go rigid again and tried to calm down in the mix. Kiara kissed me on the cheek and the action caused me to shiver.

"I love you, Johnny," she whispered. "Thank you."

Her words caused me to grin, though I was unsure of how to take them. I decided to go for the gusto, anyway.

"And I love you, Kiara. More than you know."

We pulled apart, eyes still on each other as the DJ announced the surprise entertainment for the night. Not even five seconds later, the first notes of Fuckin' with Me dropped and Kiara's whole disposition changed.

"You. Didn't?!" she screamed as Tank emerged from behind the curtain of the stage.

The aforementioned called for the birthday girl and I'd been all but forgotten as she rushed to the stage. She was at the front singing along, screaming missing lyrics when he paused to sing along with everybody else. I grinned hard, enjoying her having fun as if I'd thrown the party for myself.

Xander joined me in the VIP section, throwing an arm around my shoulder while he held a drink of his own in the other. I laughed, already knowing my friend was about to talk his nonsense.

"Man listen. She better be calling you King-ding-a-ling-you-run-the-universe-and-this-pussy by the end of the night or I'm fighting her myself."

"Shut the fuck up, Xander."

"Nah son, for real!"

I shrugged. "She's happy, I'm happy."

It was as simple as that. Kiara was my heart either way.

"I mean, don't get me wrong. I ain't shit and you know this ain't my movement. Kiara's a good woman though and she deserved this. My man Julien been fumbling for years so fuck it. I'm just glad you stopped being a bitch and made a move. I'll still fight her, though."

I shoved at my friend as he laughed and then started to follow behind a chick that passed right by our section. I shook my head at how easily he fell prey to women but turned my attention back to Kiara acting up as she watched Tank perform. I went back to the thought that I was happy she was happy. I still couldn't ignore that my heart hung in the balance and this party was my grand gesture of letting her know I wanted her. I hadn't only thrown this party for her because I was that good of a guy.

If she went back to Julien after this however, I might have to fight her myself as well.

Chapter Three

Kiara David

I wasn't used to being at the tail end of any party. Still, at the end of it all, Johnathan was thanking people for coming out and I was looking up at him, starry eyed at the fact that he truly went out of his way to throw a party...for me.

I took in all the flowers that filled up the space in various shades of blue. Royal blue, Robin's Egg Blue, Tiffany Blue, Powder blue. Blue was my favorite color and Johnathan delivered. Balloons in blue were everywhere. My sash and my dress matched most of the décor and perfectly contrasted it, so my pictures were amazing.

I was still speechless at the fact that Tank was in the same space as I was, singing my favorite selections from different albums. Pictures of me with the legendary singer are now in my possession, thanks to my best friend.

I melted at the thought, knowing the title didn't suit him anymore. Not after I saw the way he looked at me, naked with longing. I couldn't even deny the truth that I had seen for years, even when others tried to point out the fact. I couldn't even deny the truth that I loved him. It was obvious that the games had to end tonight.

The last few minutes of the party left me gratefully hugging Shaunte and thanking her for her efforts in throwing the party with Johnathan. I knew while Johnathan had the idea, Shaunte was the one executing the vision. I'd know her touch on an event anywhere. Still, even for her this was amazing and moved my heart in such a way that healed me.

After the grateful tears, Shaunte´ and Micah left hand-in-hand after telling us they'd see us around. Johnathan turned to me, asking me what I wanted to do next.

My answer had been to hold out my hand to him and tell him to lead the way. We walked amicably through the hotel's halls, but I hadn't missed him rubbing his thumb across my hand. The small action caused my heart to skip a beat and look up at him as we talked about the high points of my party. We took the elevator up to the rooftop and picked a secluded area toward the front.

We passed through the crowd that was well into their own party and I melted as I reveled into the pressure of Johnathan's hand covering mine. Our shift was barely noticeable but it was there. His thumb was still caressing the top of my hand. I was following him and admiring the long lines of his back in the outfit he wore.

It'd been a simple study of black on black. The only color was in the blue boutonniere on his shirt and the golden buckle of his belt. It would've been a sexier scene if I weren't still gushing about the party.

We slowed down to a more secluded place on the rooftop and I took in the skyline, idly playing around with the idea of moving out. Brooklyn was calling my name. It was building up to be the next Manhattan for years and I was ready to settle in before gentrification totally settled in, making living in New York even more difficult than it already was. I thought about the possibilities of doing it for a little while.

It was amazing what one person's kindness did to your psyche.

I'd gone back to relaying my happiness to Johnathan when he pulled me into a bear hug, his laughter coming from deep in his belly. A kiss on top of my forehead was his response as my hands rested on top of his.

"You got me for real, Johnny," I sighed. "I had no clue this was coming..."

"I was shocked I didn't confess. I'm not good at keeping things from you."

Which was true. That was both a pro and a con in our friendship. Things that should have been kept quiet; Johnathan told me. Things that needed to be said to me, Johnathan was good at ripping the bandaid off. For once, my friend held it down although I knew it pained him not to say anything earlier when I called him in tears.

Still, it was finally time to address something that I could no longer keep quiet about. The pink elephant that was our love had been looming around long enough.

"...except the fact that you're in love with me."

I turned my body to him and looked him in the eye. His expression was suddenly sheepish, and he shrugged helplessly. I started to giggle, not expecting that reaction. He shook his head and I waited silently, as I'd thrown down the gauntlet.

"I am," he said, quietly. "I have been for years. Still, I was hesitant to say something."

"Why?"

"There's always a chance you didn't want to take things further. We been friends for years. I know on some level you loved this nigga or else it would've been easier to step in years ago."

"Johnny...how long?"

He smirked. "Oh, you care now? You knew I was in love with you for years and you stayed."

"What did you expect from me, John? Did I truly know or was I just supposed to listen to the boys and dump my boyfriend for you? Especially when you didn't show me we were anything other than friends?"

Johnathan opened his mouth and closed it, his defense lost on that simple fact. Of course, the attraction was there because he was a man, I was a woman, and we were close. Still, I was never leaving based on hints and desires. That wasn't smart in my opinion. I grew up with Johnathan and my band of boys and one thing they consistently taught me was that if a man wants you, he shows you. That was without fail. There were ways Johnathan showed me he loved me as his friend but as a woman?

Not until this very moment.

"Besides, one thing my mama made sure to teach me was that I should never approach a man. I don't care if you walked around butt naked with a neon sign on that said you loved me. How do I know if you never say anything? Besides, you and Xander were the tag team of the century back at Clark..."

Johnathan laughed, shaking his head at my last point but he couldn't deny it.

"You're right."

He reached for my hands and pulled me in closer. Tilting up my face to him I looked into his eyes and found myself biting my lip as suddenly, I felt the energy he was giving me. I felt his love. I felt his lust. I felt his need.

"Kiara...they were all consolation prizes in your wake. Some of them might've been a worthy partner but...I wanted you. I had to come to grips with that. I didn't want to ruin our friendship."

"So, what inspired...all of this?"

"Me realizing that I needed to stop pussyfooting around and take what's mine."

Johnathan pulled me into him, flush against him and I felt myself melt into him. It was like coming home from a long day and finally kicking my shoes off. It was like settling into a hot bath with aching muscles. A shiver ran through me as I felt his hands acutely, holding both sides of my waist. I was suddenly filled with need for him like I never had before, and I found myself biting my lip in want. Looking into his eyes overwhelmed me so I looked away.

A quiet moan escaped me as he leaned in, laying kisses on the left side of my face. I granted him access as he kissed lower, slowly from my jaw down to my shoulders. He pulled away, doing the same motions on the other side and my excitement rose. I slid my arms around his neck and melted even more when he pulled back to look into my eyes.

"Johnny..."

"Yes, Key?"

His voice was deeper than I'd ever heard it and it caused me to swallow.

"I love you, Johnny."

"You love me, Key?"

His hand slid up to my neck, his thumb caressing my cheek. He looked lovingly into my eyes and suddenly nothing else mattered. That ache that had been my friend for years suddenly packed its bags and vacated my soul. Suddenly nothing about the moment was comfortable for said ache that had been by my side through loneliness. The ache that had been there, even when I was in a room full of people. Even when I was in the throes of passion with my actual boyfriend.

Suddenly, there was a fullness I'd never known. The only other ache that remained was the one that longed for the moment I was experiencing now. The sweetness that bloomed in my heart was one I was growing fond of.

"Yes. For years. In high school when I wasn't even sure you were looking at me at all."

Another smirk as his thumb kept caressing my cheek.

"Who could miss you, Kiara David? You switched out those baggy pants for high waisted ones. Your shirts started fitting you. Your hair started being done. I was around a diamond in the rough every day and was upset when everybody else started noticing."

"That was your fault, Mr. Barnes," I giggled. "You were the one who waited, and I know you were telling everybody you didn't see me that way."

Jonathan smirked, neither confirming or denying what I knew to be true.

"Either way, I was looking. Been looking. Been wanting. I want you, now."

Johnathan tilted my head and began to lean in. Before his lips connected, he paused, looking into my eyes.

"May I, baby?"

"You may."

His hand slid into my hair as our lips connected. We groaned, as we kissed once, twice, and then once more. I opened my mouth to grant him entrance and became putty in his hands. I wasn't sure how long we kissed, only that when we parted, we went back in and kissed again. It was easily becoming addictive in a way I never imagined, and all it did was stoke the flames because I wanted more.

I found myself smiling hard when Johnathan pulled away to look in my face. His smile mirrored mine.

"Would it be rude to ask if you want to spend the night with me?"

"No."

Johnathan reached out for my hand and led me away from the rooftop. We walked toward the elevator and made the ascent to a room he already reserved.

We stepped through the door after he opened it. The door barely closed behind us before his lips had been on mine again. This time his kiss was insistent and full of the want he spoke of. I trembled as his hands started to both slowly and efficiently undress me right where we stood by the door.

My breasts were on full display and Johnathan leaned in to take one in his mouth. My moans were shameless as he caressed the other in his hand, tweaking my nipple just right while he licked the other. I was surprised when he took his time, switching sides and giving the other breast the same attention. He pulled back and kissed all over my chest while he held my breasts in his hands, still rubbing over my nipples and making me clench down below. He continued, kissing all the way up to my neck, nuzzling his face in the crook of it and kissing me in a spot to make me weak.

"Johnny..."

I moaned for him, the delicious torture only a pre-requisite. I suddenly wanted what I craved for many nights. Even being with another man, Johnathan lived between us, and I wondered if Julien felt that much and decided not to care in the slightest after a time. I wasn't sure but also didn't want to lose the moment by living in another moment.

"Yes baby...what you want?"

He pulled down my dress further, kissing along my body as more skin was revealed. He kneeled as he reached my vagina, and I heard him groan as it was revealed to him. Leaning in again, he kissed it, parting it and using his tongue to lick the bundle of nerves. He did so languorously, causing me to gasp and reach blindly for the wall behind me.

"This what you want, baby?"

I nodded as he went back to work. My knees were starting to give out and before I could start forming words that I couldn't keep standing, Johnathan paused. Picking me up, he walked the short distance to the bed and sat me down. He undid the shoes I wore, tossing one after the other. He looked up at me as he'd done so.

"Forgive me, baby. I have better manners than that. Reaching for dessert when I haven't even washed up for dinner yet."

I blushed as he leaned up to kiss my lips again. I fell into the kiss.

"I'm not mad, baby."

Johnathan pulled the rest of my dress down and then proceeded to undress himself. I found my mouth watering as his shirt hit the floor. I decided to get comfortable as I watched my greatest birthday gift unwrap himself. His arms like iron cannons were on full display. His broad shoulders, his chest all looked as if a sculptor fashioned him without sleep. Nothing but determination and inspiration to bring forth perfection. He dropped his pants and underwear and my eyes widened. I had many assumptions but what was in front of me shocked me. My current-actually-ex-boyfriend-wasn't a slacker. Still, Johnathan was both long, thick, and curved. He swung a little to the left and I was amazed at how heavy it looked.

"You look excited, Key."

I giggled, watching as he walked towards the bed, crawling toward me. Another kiss was shared. It was slow and unhurried. I reached down and gripped him as we kissed, and I enjoyed his moan. The very thought that he was moaning for me excited me. My legs parted as he reached down to play with me as well.

"I am."

"Hm. Well, let me finish this dessert."

And he had. Kissing along my body he did so achingly slowly. It was reverent the way his lips pressed against my skin. I felt gloried. I felt adored. I felt loved.

He spread my legs and went back to work. I watched him as he put every bit of his energy into my center. I became ice cream as he licked me, falling into my middle with his tongue. He kissed my lips and flicked my bud until I was crying his name. My legs sat on top of his shoulders, and he reached long arms for my breasts. He tweaked my nipples, sending electricity shooting back down to where he was giving no quarter. He hummed as my pleasure flowed into his mouth and hitting the precipice, I came for him.

Johnathan pulled back, watching me as I came down from my rapture and gave me a hard grin. I watched him stand up, snatching up his pants and pulling out the tell-tale golden wrapper. I breathed, reclaiming air into my lungs that I lost as he sheathed himself, returning to me.

"You ready for me, baby? This night about to be long."

I parted my legs for him, kissing him in reply. Johnathan pushed inside of me, inch by inch and the profanity that left his thick lips let me know he was about to make good on his promise.

Life as I had known it before would never be the same and for that, I was grateful.

Johnathan Barnes

Kiara was sobbing my name and it felt like I got harder each and every time. Something about my name on her lips turned me on and made me weak. I hadn't known until the moment I was thrusting in and out of her that it was always the case. I was hearing her now in her purest form however, declaring she wanted me, and it made me wish I'd taken her from this man sooner. Still, everything had its place in time.

She was on all fours for me while I held her by her slim waist, hitting hard. I'd already gone easy earlier but something about her passion stirred me until I just couldn't hold back. The way she welcomed it surprised me but again, I should've known better. She always liked it rough from when we met. My love was a tomboy and hadn't been for the softer life until she met an enthusiast in Shaunte. I was grateful that she reminded my love that she was indeed a woman. That she was a miracle and a gift. One that I would love and protect my whole life long.

I was like a freight train in her wetness, and I took more and more of her. And she gave to me without abandon. I wondered if I was making up for lost time or punishing her for it but decided I was just happy I was finally getting it. I knew I had to make it count in case she changed her mind. I'd always have the memory...of every thrust. Of every inch of her. Of every ounce. I wanted to swallow her whole and get every bit.

"Baby, don't stop. Please don't stop..."

I groaned, leaning into her shoulder. I kissed her lips and pulled her ear into my mouth, delighting in the shivers that ran down her spine while I worked her.

"I'm not stopping, baby. Not until you've had enough."

I bit into her shoulder and told her how good she tasted. I then pulled her up against my chest, sliding my hand upwards to her neck, adding just enough pressure. Her gasp told me she liked the silent claim I was putting on her.

"This pussy soaking my dick like it always knew it was mine..." I growled. "You hear that?"

"Mmm...yes!"

I continued, holding her up even when her legs began to tremble. I reached down with one hand and began to massage her, express shipping her orgasm. My efforts had been rewarded with her crying my name as she came. She pulsated around me, causing me to groan. I gave into my own orgasm, cursing the good feelings because I hadn't been ready to finish yet.

Kiara whimpered as I pulled out of her. I laid her down gently, all the finesse I was lacking earlier in my movements. I'd gotten rid of the barrier that was between us and then crawled back on the huge king-sized bed, pulling her into my arms. She smiled, pure joy directed at me, and I was helpless but to smile back. Our hands linked with the easiness of a couple that's been together for many years versus our mere moments. I randomly kissed her shoulder every now and again.

Kiara turned around and I was rewarded with looking into her pretty face. Seeing all the love she had for me out in the open hit me so hard I was grateful that I was lying down. She leaned up to kiss me, her full lips causing me to groan. I pulled at her leg and sat it across my waist. I palmed her backside and leaned in, pulling her bottom lip into my mouth, biting down lightly. Her answering sigh came out shaky and I swallowed a chuckle, knowing what I was doing to her.

"You're turning me on again."

Her voice was raspy, and the timbre caused me to stiffen.

"I'm not doing anything."

Kiara leaned in to kiss the side of my mouth and I massaged her generous backside. Seconds later I sharply smacked it and watched as she quivered. My baby loved being loved on, but she also liked being manhandled... respectfully.

"You are and you know it."

She reached in between us, stroking me. I became stone in her hands almost immediately. I groaned, leaning in to kiss her. I slid my tongue down her throat and the melody of her moan delighted me.

"Damn, baby. I can listen to you on repeat."

"I was thinking the same about you."

Another kiss. Another followed that one. I was pulling her hand away to pause her because I was ready all over again. I reached for a second condom and wrapped up. I saw my baby bite her lower lip, excited to receive me all over again and chuckled.

Her cell phone interrupted our interlude. Recognition lit in her eyes, and I could tell Julien was calling her for the first time at all. I felt my face harden because of the lack of care. It was easy to see the non-apology in his movements. Somewhere along the way, he honestly didn't care how he hurt Kiara and it was both disheartening and embarrassing in my opinion as a man. Once you realized that you didn't care, it was time to step aside. I understood that my love had her part to play in it all but as for him, he was the type that just didn't want to see her move on. Her having to move on was too much work that he wasn't in the mood to go through.

They built a life together. At some point I knew he was thinking of marriage but only because of the time he invested into her. I knew in his mind she made the perfect wife but not because he loved her. The woman he loved was always with him. I was unsure of when it happened, but he withheld his love from her and gave it to another. It was sloppy business on his behalf. I believe that because of their history he just didn't want to lose the comfort of her being in his corner. Still, Kiara deserved more than one-sided love and it was high time he learned that much.

"You going to get that?"

I had to ask the question, mostly because I wasn't standing in the way of whatever she had going on. She confessed that she loved me but again, my heart was in the balance until she let me know for sure.

Kiara reached up to stroke my neck.

"Oh, Johnny...I'd only be picking up the phone for my man at this hour."

"That so?"

My smile spread. Kiara's face frowned thoughtfully as she leaned up to kiss my lips once more. The phone was still ringing in the background as she ran her hands up and down my back. I felt myself weaken for her, even as her reassurance made me want to beat my chest like I was Tarzan.

"You're right here, aren't you, Johnny?"

"That I am...doing what I'm supposed to do to you at this hour..."

I slid inside of her on that note. Her reception of me was so sweet, it was all I could do not to tear her all the way up again from jump. As it were, it hadn't taken too long. Julien called about five more times in the midst of me making love to my woman. The ringtone was only the background to Kiara screaming my name in loving desperation.

I'd awaken to gazing upon Kiara's beautiful face once more as she slept on my chest. My heart was happy to finally make claim on the one I loved and I silently promised to make every moment worth her while, even as I ran my fingers through her hair. My ministrations caused her to awaken and smile as she took me in after only a second's confusion. She giggled as she leaned up to kiss my lips in greeting. I groaned, returning her affections.

"I'm hungry, baby."

I grinned, wanting to make a crude joke about working her out but instead suggested we head to breakfast. Her agreement caused us to find our way to the shower to take a quick one and then make our next move.

Before dawn totally took over the city, we checked out. I was ready to take her to breakfast and then present her with my actual birthday gift to her which was a shopping spree.

The aim had been to totally spoil her rotten like she'd never been spoiled. I was excited to see the look on her face when she saw me pull my card out.

I talked about Uriel but I, myself, had to admit that I was a fool over Kiara. A plum fool.

I drove through Brooklyn with one hand on the wheel and the other holding onto hers. It was a quiet, comfortable ride that soothed me after an eventful night.

I slowed up to her house, thinking I was also one kind of motherfucker to pull up to a woman's house after I wore her out the night before with her "man" waiting. I knew with the shoe on the other foot I wouldn't have taken the disrespect.

As it were, we noticed most of Kiara's belongings strewn all over the lawn.

"What the fuck?!"

I slowed down just enough for her to hop out of the car. I decided to get out and lean against the door to keep watch. I could already tell Julien was out of his mind and if I needed to step in, I would. It didn't take much for him to figure out her disappearance was the ultimate sin to him, and he was ready to be rid of her completely. Or, rather, he was ready to see me. He didn't have an actual excuse before and now I supplied him with one.

So, I was ready.

I watched as Kiara tried to open her house door but like magic, the locks were changed. I felt my face harden at that plot twist. I watched my love bang on the door, insulted at the audacity of her ex and I frowned up my face, feeling much the same way. His reaction after one slight was equal to what hers should have been after many. Sometimes that's the thanks you get after giving a man a long leash.

"Look at what the cat dragged in! You're looking beautiful, baby."

The door finally opened and Julien appeared. He was clearly drunk. I sighed, hoping I didn't have to put him to sleep.

"Julien, what the hell is going on?"

Julien leaned against the door with his arms crossed. Laughter was on his lips but it was arrogant, like he carried a secret only he had access to. I fought against the urge to step up to the clown and give him the fight he's been looking for.

"You tell me. You leave the house. Don't call. Don't text. Don't pick up when I call you. Now you're back here acting all lost with good ole Johnny Boy leaning up the side of the car like he's going to do something. You think I'm stupid, Kiara?"

Kiara crossed her arms in retaliation. "Be that as it may, Julien, I deserve better than for you to toss all my shit on the fucking lawn. You've done way worse, and I forgave it."

"That was on you, shorty. If you were really that upset, you should've been left. I know my boy Barnes has been waiting for his shot for years and you finally gave him some pussy. I'm thinking you wasn't with it all this time, but a nigga miss your birthday and you happily fuck the next dude."

"Julien. You missed it for years. I should've been left."

He smirked, unmoved by anything Kiara was saying to him. All he saw was that she cheated. None of his sins mattered in the grand scheme. It was Kiara's one sin that made him feel he was righteous in the moves he was making.

"I hear you, but you're not going to sit on somebody else's dick and think you're going to keep living here. I want you out."

Kiara opened and closed her mouth. Suddenly, I watched her go calm and shrug her shoulders.

"Give me a week and I'm gone."

I didn't miss the surprise in Julien's face. He expected her to beg. He humiliated her so she would cry and beg. I knew had she done so he would've forgiven her. If she promised to stay away from me, he would've even let her move back in and act like it never happened...that is, until he wanted to bring it up to humble her.

"You have three days. You take longer than that, I'm throwing all your shit in the garbage."

I chuckled, entertained thoroughly by every move this man made. He was childish and needed the dramatics most men didn't. I was annoyed that Kiara hadn't noticed that in all these years.

Kiara pushed past him, and I stood, waiting, silently. Julien edged a look at me, and I looked back, unafraid. I wasn't sure when he thought I was ever afraid of him. I hoped he walked over here.

Wisely, he stayed put.

Kiara walked back outside with a weekend bag and Julien grabbed her arm, halting her from walking. That was when I walked up toward them. Years ago, I might've let him have that moment being that I wasn't her man. However, now that I was, I wasn't about to allow him to be handsy like it was all fine and dandy.

"I hope you don't crawl back to me once he's gotten his fill of you. You think he loves you when he was just waiting his turn."

Kiara looked up at Julien with a smile that didn't reach her eyes.

"I promise you with my whole heart, Julien, I won't be back. Not after this."

She snatched her arm from his, walking toward me. She stopped short, not expecting me to be as close as I was. I took her bag and motioned for her to wait for me in the car. Julien kept his eyes on me, affronted that I stood in his space with my gaze pinned on him. My anger couldn't be hidden and no longer was I in the mood to keep myself in check for the lowlife standing in front of me.

"Real quick, you made your point clear but let that be the last time you lay a hand on her."

"Get the fuck outta my face, Barnes. Your thirsty ass been waiting for your turn this whole time, you got it now, have fun while it lasts. You think she's someone worth having but it's not really all that."

"I don't remember giving a fuck about your opinion. I didn't ask yours when you were doing you, Smith. I kept it G the whole time until you made it apparent that you don't care anymore."

Julien snarled at me, "I oughta punch you in the mouth, nigga."

I smiled hard, pulled my hand back and did exactly to him what he wanted to do to me. His surprise was evident as he reached up and found blood on his hand where his mouth was split. I smirked when he snarled and then attempted to rush me. Another nicely placed uppercut landed, forcing him to stumble back and fall in front of his door. Walking up to him once more, I spat.

"Like I said, that's me now. Keep your fuckin' hands to yourself. And have her shit packed up when she comes back to get it."

I walked back to the car, taking deep breaths to calm myself before I slid back in. I took a moment to open the back door and put Kiara's weekender in the back and then got in my front seat. I sighed, reaching over and pulling her face to mine so I could look into her eyes. My question was silent and without fail, she knew what was on my mind.

"I'm fine, Johnny." she questioned, "Are you?"

I nodded, "I want to hop back out and finish beating his ass."

Kiara giggled, leaning in to kiss my lips.

"No. Let's go eat. It's been hours and I need something. Somebody burned all the calories I had left."

I slid a look over at her and chuckled as I pulled out of the spot I took up. I felt myself calm when Kiara reached for my hand, linking our fingers together. I didn't even realize I was upset before then.

"So, what do you want to do about your stuff?"

"I hadn't been planning on thinking about it," Kiara shrugged. "I figured I'd just call some movers and pack it up into storage. I knew I was going to move out anyway."

"Hm. I'll pay for it. You can stay with me."

I felt Kiara stiffen a little bit as I slowed to a red light. I looked over, realizing she was uncomfortable. I sighed, running a thumb over her hand.

"Baby."

She looked up at me as I pulled off once the light turned green.

"If you don't want to stay with me, let me know. I'm wired to take care of you, Key. You know that."

She squeezed tighter, acknowledging me silently.

"I know," she said, softly. "I'm still getting used to the fact that we're together."

I slowed at another light and turned to her, smirking at the vulnerability in her eyes. It didn't slip my mind that she pretty much walked away from a twelve-year relationship to be with me. The change hadn't been more than twelve hours between us yet.

Still, I leaned in and kissed her softly on the lips. Kiara melted into me as I kissed her once and then twice more.

"I love you. We're transitioning so there might be moments where I might become too much. You have to let me know."

Kiara nodded, returning my kiss with one of her own. I was tempted to deepen the kiss when a car horn blared at us.

The light was green, and I chuckled at the fact that you could always find an angry New Yorker at any hour of the day or night.

I'd been thinking about the possibilities this change could have on her but hadn't thought about what it might mean for me as well.

Chapter Four

Kiara David

A few hours later saw me at the mall with Lashawn and Shaunte´. We shopped amicably as I swiped Johnathan's AMEX without a care in the world. I was filled with glee, almost as if the past few hours hadn't happened.

My man presented me with his card, gifting me with a shopping spree for my physical birthday gift. I hadn't fathomed he had more past the party, my new dress, and our time together and I'd been grateful. His AMEX being pressed into my hand with specific instructions not to go past three thousand made me emotional. I almost passed the card back to him, but he anticipated me, pressing it back into my hands and laying a kiss on me that rocked my world.

"I spoil mine, there's no reason for you to be worried about spending my money. I'm not worried about getting into those guts..."

Which was true. Another session erupted between us when we returned to his house. That was the reason I ended up meeting with my girls late afternoon instead of early as we'd originally planned.

Our time together had been comfortable and quaint until we settled into Cheesecake Factory a few hours later.

I realized Shaunte and Lashawn wore salacious grins and I knew what time it was. They wanted details that I'd been slow to come up off of. I was still going to play coy, however. I wasn't exactly ready to speak about Johnathan and me yet. I was enjoying the feeling of keeping it between us.

Still, once the three of us had given our drink orders to the waitress, not even twenty seconds passed by when Lashawn went for the jugular.

"Bitch, we know you fucked John last night. Details or you're paying for lunch."

I laughed helplessly, not thinking Lashawn would be the one to bring it up. Also, I hadn't imagined her going so hard. She giggled when I said that much.

"Y'all stressed my baby out over this dumb shit for years. Now I need to know if it happened or not after he went through the pains to finally say he loved you."

I hung my head low, thinking of Uriel and how he'd tried to vouch for Johnathan throughout the years. Though I respected my friend highly for trying to make things happen, I couldn't accept his word. Every now and again, Xander and Micah would try to stir the pot. I told them both to stop being messy and let life happen. I could tell across the board they'd been annoyed with the fact that I stayed with Julien. I knew I should've left a long time ago.

The realization came while I was tearfully complaining to Johnathan that Julien only wanted our relationship to work in his favor and not for me at all. While he was capable of love, he wasn't capable of doing what was necessary to keep me happy. Alternatively, I did everything in my power to keep him happy, even when he was at his lowest.

"I know," I said, lowly. "He knew there wasn't much I could do with what he gave me."

"Yeah, but damn Key!"

Lashawn was laughing and I knew in her mind it was that easy for me to dump Julien and just walk into Johnathan's arms, but it wasn't. Shaunte knew that much better than anyone being that we went to school together. She knew the pecking order for the most part. Johnathan hadn't done much while we were in high school but college? Like I mentioned before, he and Xander were a tag team. I wasn't going to risk what I had for whatever phase of life Johnathan was in.

"It's been a long time coming. I'm guilty of feeling frustrated as well. You two were hard to watch...but I blame Johnathan more."

Lashawn sucked her teeth. "Not when she knew this nigga was in love."

"You expected me to leave Julien, too? Based on what, Lashawn?"

My laughter was helpless but mostly because I hadn't known Lashawn was frustrated. I was just now realizing it or rather she was just now letting it be known.

"Based on your knowledge. Based on knowing Julien was a piece of shit for years. Hell sis, I honestly just wanted better for you. You only stayed because y'all had time invested. After a while it was very obvious you loved this nigga. Got him playing boyfriend number two when he was boyfriend number one the whole time."

I wasn't sure where she'd gotten the boyfriend number two thoughts from, unless it was from Uriel. Jonathan and I had close calls but nothing of note happened. Julien knew to appear when things started to get shaky. Either that or Johnathan stepped away before it could happen. I'd be further left confused when I saw him walking around with a new face right after the fact.

"John was my best friend. The stakes of dating your best friend are high, especially when he wasn't on shit at the time."

"I mean...on both sides y'all were tripping, but Johnathan let it go on for too long. He could've intercepted years ago and didn't. It was obvious that had he walked up to you and told you to drop Julien you would have."

The waitress walked up to us, placing our drinks on coasters, and walked away as quietly as she appeared. I picked up my drink and took a sip, enjoying the flavors and saving face from the accurate summation Shaunte laid out for me.

"You don't know me."

"Au contraire. I know you well. I don't blame you for staying your position. John should've manned up and made his play years ago. I watched him deal with women he didn't even want when all he had to say was enough. I guess he finally had enough because he called me like, Shaun, I need a party and I'm willing to spend that bread. So, I'm proud of him."

Lashawn smirked, still pinning me with her gaze and shrugged. "I guess. Like I said, details or you paying."

I smiled and lightly kicked Lashawn's leg. Although she'd always been in the mix, I only recently started hanging out with Lashawn. Once she and Uriel met it was pretty much forever for them both. I adored her, seeing how she made my friend a happy man.

"Well, we finally confessed last night. I lowkey pressed Johnathan but he basically asked me what I wanted to do about it?"

"Oh?"

We pulled back once our salads were served. We took a short moment to pray before continuing the conversation.

"Yeah," I answered, with a helpless smile. "We ended up making out. Next thing I know..."

I trailed off for effect, forcing Lashawn's face to bloom into a beautiful smile. She squealed as she stabbed into her salad and took a bite. She chewed thoughtfully and methodically, and it caused me to take a bite of my own.

"Oh?" Shaunte's eyebrows raised. "You're glowing though. I assume he knew what to do."

My friend cackled and forced me to bump her with my shoulder. I nodded but didn't elaborate much. Something about our love seemed so...intimate. The thought of airing things out like a teenager didn't sit well. Years ago, I blabbed about my first time with Julien. There'd been bravado and excitement because I'd grabbed onto a man that mostly every woman lusted over. This was wholly different. In ways I didn't even totally understand yet, but this wasn't that situation. I didn't want to share Johnathan with anybody.

"He..." I sighed. "He knew just what to do. I'm leaving it at that."

I'm sure the fact that I was blushing told enough of a story. Lashawn nodded, the look on her face pleased. Shaunte laughed before taking another bite of her salad.

"Again, I'm proud of him. My only question is what happens to Julien?"

That part, I was ready to write a tell-all book about.

"Julien pretty much figured it out when I didn't pick up my phone at three in the morning. And then John pulled up with me in the car trying to do a quick in and out of the house."

Lashawn's eyes widened, along with Shaunte's and both of them started snickering. I shrugged helplessly.

"Dag. He couldn't even let you cheat in peace?!" Shaunte squealed. "What he say?!"

"Fuck what he said, Shaun. That nigga had all of my clothes all over the lawn! I'm so surprised nobody pulled up and took anything!"

"What the fuck?!" Lashawn squealed, "How dare he?!"

Shaun's face read horror when she said, "So, he couldn't be bothered to even call to say Happy Birthday, buy a gift, hell even deliver some dick but he got time to throw all your shit out of the house you helped him get? Am I hearing this correctly?"

I nodded, "You are. After helping that piece of shit get back on his feet after he was being pitiful after messing up his career. After he cheated time and again. Instead of letting me go in peace he wants to act like I was the worst he's ever had."

I started to tremble again at the memory. Lashawn's face read contempt as I told the story from the start to finish. She shook her head as our entrees arrived.

"Should've let John beat the brakes off that nigga. Y'all good. I just know L would have..."

"And did."

"Oop!" Lashawn said, "I'm shocked nobody pressed charges."

I shrugged, "I don't really know what was said after John told me to get in the car. Julien grabbed me on my way back out the door telling me some dumb shit about 'don't come crawling back to him once Johnathan's had his fill.'"

"Hm." Shaunte said, "I don't think Julien understood that the pecking order has changed. My homeboy is not about to be polite anymore. Those days are over."

"Too bad you didn't pick up the phone so he could hear y'all last night. That would've been a good time."

We busted out laughing at the thought while we ate. I nodded my agreement, wishing I had as well but grateful I hadn't stooped that low. Men were good for doing to a woman what they couldn't handle being done to them. I couldn't count how many times Julien embarrassed me. That's why the dramatic scene outside of our house last night didn't make sense.

"Textbook narcissism," Shaunte said. "We hate to see it. So, you're moving in with John?"

I shook my head in the negative and both of them had twin looks of shock all over them.

"I'm going to stay with him for a little while but...right now I need space. I just got out of a twelve-year relationship. We just got together last night. I know we have history but...it's a huge change between us. I need to adjust, and he needs to as well. And me knowing my man..."

I trailed off, the phrase foreign on my lips. My two friends smiled brightly, knowing that I was referring to Johnathan. I flushed, all of it slightly overwhelming to talk about.

"I know you better claim that man, sis," Lashawn said, giggling. "Blushing and shit..."

Shaunte giggled. "What were you saying, Key?"

I rolled my eyes. "I know Johnathan and he's not even going to realize how much is going to change between us. He's going to think it's still a bomb ass best friendship, plus sex."

"Isn't that what the best relationships are?" Shaunte questioned. "You're losing me."

"Yeah but...I don't know him as a man. Only as my best friend. I got to know him intimately last night but...you know."

"I get it."

Lashawn replied, nodding her head. I was surprised that Shaunte couldn't relate but her and Micah's situation had been different.

They'd shared a friendship through middle school, then freshman year of high school, Micah stepped up to the plate and told Shaunte he wanted to be with her. I was surprised that my friend agreed. In my opinion, I felt she was more Uriel's speed. Then again, looking back I realized they would've been a train wreck. Mostly because Shaunte was dramatic as the day was long, though she was smart as a whip. Micah wasn't much different. I just thought she'd go for a quieter guy.

They wouldn't have been friends for as long as me and Johnathan were. There weren't patterns to break out of. There weren't conversations to skip over and save for the girls. It didn't hit me for a time, but the guys were now my opposition in a sense. I was now...on the normal side of the fence as it stood. I was no longer the cool girl with all the best guy friends at her beck and call. I said that much to Shaunte, and she smiled wide.

"Yes, my dear. You're growing up. It's about time."

I sighed as I enjoyed the rest of my time with the girls. I was learning more and more to lean into my femininity, but some moments were painful. I suppose growing up isn't always easy. That much I'd find out in time.

Johnathan Barnes

I watched Kiara step outside of Queens Center Mall, grinning wide as she saw me parked across the street. I leaned against my car, a smile of my own face present as she walked toward me, bags in both of her hands. Her almond dark brown eyes creased just a bit from her grin. Her full lips made my own ache to kiss them and her perfectly round nose sat in the center, making my heart melt. Her slim, petite frame was clothed in a white two-piece set, a biker short and a bralette. She wore an oversized beige button down. On her feet were beige and white New Balance sneakers. Watching her walk to me left me in awe at how both adorable and sexy she was at the same time.

I relieved her of her bags once I popped open my trunk and placed the bags inside. After I finished doing that, I relieved the ache that had grown by pulling her in for a kiss. I grabbed a handful of her backside, taking another kiss from her. I pulled away to see her blushing.

"I missed you too, Johnny."

Her eyes were heavy lidded as she took in my gaze and I chuckled. I took her hand and led her over to the passenger side, opening the door. I helped her in and then shut the door, returning to my side. I drove off toward my home not long after.

Our ride was quiet but comfortable. Her hand rested in mine while I drove through the BQE, slowly making my way back to Brooklyn and into Bed-Stuy. About an hour later, I felt my smile pull as I came up on the brownstone that belonged to me. I was in the mix of renovating the lower floor for rental income, but my upper level was finished. I was grateful for the career that I enjoyed that afforded my lifestyle. It hadn't been the thing to keep me from talking to Kiara, but it all came together around the same time I'd grown tired of her being with Julien for real.

I slowed the car down, parking in my spot. I hopped out after turning off the engine and walking straight to the back. Kiara popped out of the car, following me with a slower gait. When she reached me, I'd already had her bags out of the trunk.

"Might as well walk up the stairs now, baby," I smirked. "Fake helpful ass."

Kiara giggled as she walked next to me.

"Thank you, baby."

A grin was on my face as I stopped short at my front door. I juggled the bags, searched for the keys and handed them to Kiara. She slid the keys in and opened the door, walking in first. I followed behind her, allowing my door to slam and called for my woman who was trying to disappear into the bathroom.

"What?" she giggled. "I'll handle them, just leave them in the living room."

I rolled my eyes and placed her bags in the living room and continued my walk. I asked Kiara if she'd eaten and she replied that she had. I then wondered whether I was ready to eat for real or eat my girlfriend out. Either was a good idea to me.

I decided to run a bath for us. In my opinion Kiara had been gone too long, and I just wanted to relax with her in my arms. I also meant to make love to her a little later so I figured we might as well just wash the world off both of us.

I walked up to the second floor, past my master bedroom and to the bathroom, walking over the heated tiles to the freestanding tub in the middle. It sat nearby the window, allowing for light to flood in with no abandon. I ran a bath, pouring in Epsom salt and some light bubbles. Of course, I did that more for Kiara. I reminded myself to keep some rose petals around for when I really meant to turn up the romance.

I checked my linen closet for some towels and threw them in my towel warmer. I played with the idea of grabbing some fruit and champagne and remembered I didn't have either, so I settled on water.

I bumped into Kiara on the way back and smiled at the quizzical look on her face.

"What are you up to?"

"We're about to take a bath."

"We?"

I placed the cups of water on the counter and turned around to see Kiara walking in. She smiled slowly.

"This part of the birthday experience, too?"

I smirked. "No, this regular."

I stripped, tossing my clothes in my hamper. Kiara stripped, hesitating to do the same. I sucked my teeth, walking up to her and quietly taking the clothes out of her hands. I tossed them in and walked up to her. I leaned in, pressing my lips softly to her lips. I tried to keep it chaste because I knew more action would result in more action.

"Come here, baby, relax. You're thinking too hard."

Kiara smirked. "You don't know me."

"Hm. I know you. Bring that ass here."

I stepped in the tub first, settling in. Kiara stepped in, settling into my arms. She laid into my chest and exhaled slowly. I felt her melt against me and I wrapped my arms around her. I butterflied kisses along her face, downwards to her jaw.

"What's on your mind?"

"This feels surreal. Last night was surreal. This morning was a movie of dramatic proportions. I don't even understand how that all happened."

I chuckled. "I tried to let you handle that but once he laid his hands on you, I couldn't just stand by. I wanted to do worse but I could be putting my energies into better things."

"Like what?"

"Fucking you."

Kiara laughed softly. "I hope sex won't be our entire relationship, Johnny."

I slid my hands around her and squeezed her, laying a kiss on her cheek. The thought was hurtful, but I understood where she was coming from. However, I wouldn't buckle under her insecurity.

"I love you, Kiara. Words can't express how much I do."

"I love you, Johnny. I'm just saying-"

"-you don't want a repeat. I understand. But don't miss the fact that I spent a pretty penny on your birthday. You just spent more of my bread running through Queens Center. I'm not a man who tosses around money and honestly, no other woman got this treatment except for you. I'm a fuckin' fool over you, Key. Always have been."

"I'm sorry, baby. I do feel a lil' guilty over how we got together. I don't feel as if it were totally wrong but it's giving two wrongs don't make it right."

I chuckled. "I hear you but fuck that nigga. It's been twelve years. The truth of the matter is I should've stepped up a long time ago. I let shit rock thinking you were happy with him for a time but then I find out that you're not. I knew you loved him and hoped it would work out but overall...it just didn't. Now I'm here. I want to give you all the things he refused to. All the shit that came hard with him I'm gonna show you it's easy with me. It's not just sex. You turn me on but it's everything about you, baby. Everything."

I pulled her into me once more. Reveling in her sigh I kissed her cheek. She turned and offered me her lips and I groaned as she opened her mouth, allowing me to slide my tongue onto hers. We kissed in that position for a few moments before pulling away.

"That's one thing homeboy got right though. I have been waiting on my shot. I been waiting for him to fuck up, just like I knew he would. Now you're mine and I get to treat you like you deserve. You chose me and I'm honored."

"You're actually a smooth talker, Mr. Barnes. If I hadn't already given you some, this might've been the moment I broke."

I chuckled, linking our hands under the water.

"Hmm. So, you gonna give me that later on? I'll talk even smoother to that pussy, I promise."

Kiara giggled. "Yes, baby."

Chapter Five

Kiara David

The next morning, I found myself in Johnathan's kitchen pulling out food to make him breakfast. He was sleeping away the morning peacefully and while I missed his company, he deserved the rest after folding me up the night before. I was still floating on air and I wanted to show my appreciation.

90s R&B played in the background while I moved around, making myself fully at home in his space. Jonathan had renovated much of the brownstone with the kitchen being no exception. Everything was top of the line, including the tall Viking refrigerator and oven. He had an oversized island made with a granite top. The island itself boasted a deep soaking sink and matching food disposal. He decided to paint the walls a light green instead of leaving it colorless and I found it a nice change from the usual masculine vibe of most male appointed kitchens. There weren't any windows but the floor to ceiling doors that led to his backyard allowed in all the natural light that one wanted. It wasn't a terrible trade-off.

I decided to whip up some pancakes, eggs, and bacon for him. At the last minute I decided on home fries, so I split a potato between us.

I wondered to myself that I was doing such a thing that I hadn't done for my ex-boyfriend in years. I used to be homier and wondered what happened. I wondered if I began to get mean and pushed him away from me and then decided to stop my thought process in its tracks. I was only putting out what I'd gotten back. The way I was presently being loved made me want to cook every single meal and then serve myself up for dessert.

The past two nights made me want to put something extra in his laundry so his clothes came out both soft and smelling fresh. It made me want to make up the bed after he vacated it. It made me want...to return the love he was giving me.

I started to plate our dishes, thinking Lashawn would probably cackle if she saw me in the present moment. This was normally her domain, but it was easy to see why she went through those lengths for Uriel. My friend was a loyal lover. He was the rare man that believed in taking care of his woman and was unapologetic about spoiling her. There was no rhyme or reason. He didn't make Lashawn jump through hoops or put her through years of pain for the pleasure. I didn't say this much but though I wanted Johnathan, Uriel had been the bar I judged men by. At one point, Julien had passed the 'Uriel' test.

My friend hadn't always been an angel, but he had never been disrespectful to women. Most women never walked away from any interaction feeling used or abused. That's why I was ready to jump on his ex-girlfriend when she tried to make a play for Micah. I'd been hesitant about Lashawn when we first met but I noticed that she was besotted with him and took care of him the way he desired. So, she easily won my heart.

"Good morning, baby."

I smiled as Johnathan walked into the kitchen; his eyes were sleepy but his smile was warm as he greeted me. He cleared the distance between us and pulled me into him, kissing my lips softly. I smiled back at him, tip toeing to kissing him in return.

"Good morning, Johnny. I made you breakfast."

"I see. You're spoiling a nigga this morning."

I giggled. "Not even close. Come on before the food gets cold."

"Hmm. I thought I was going to be dining on something else when I woke up. Maybe I'll grab that for lunch."

He reached down, squeezing half of my backside. I felt my face flush as I realized he was coming on to me.

"Maybe an after-breakfast snack."

My voice had gone throaty as I felt my lust rise. I cleared my throat, pulling away from him and reaching to grab the plate that belonged to him. I heard him chuckle lightly as I had. I giggled softly, placing the plate in his hands.

"Why don't you eat? I'll join you."

His eyes swept from the top of me to the bottom and his unabashed gaze made me flush even more. Then without another word, Johnathan walked over to the dining room and began eating. I bit my lip as I grabbed my plate and followed him.

We ate quietly and amicably. Johnathan made small conversation about the work he had to embark on soon at his job.

Johnathan was a realtor. At first I thought the job wasn't for him but found it was perfect. He loved to show houses and narrate the history behind them. The neighborhood. All the stuff that people didn't like to think about as far as real estate was concerned, he was into it. I remembered him being frustrated as the new guy on the block years ago. Ten years in the field treated him well however, once he started closing deals.

"I'm getting ready to open a brokerage of my own, now," he mentioned. "I just have to start shopping for the right people for my team. And besides that, I have to take the test and that's kind of stressful."

"Kind of? You were stressed out about your license the first time."

"I was. I'll never forget that but I'm good now. It's just annoying that I have to test again."

"It's a necessary evil, baby. You'll be fine."

"I know," he said. "I'm going to make it happen, as usual."

I smiled at his bravado and continued to eat. I looked around the dining area and started to imagine the space with our children, making noise and being boisterous. I pictured a son for me and a daughter for him and another child that we'd call our bonus. I pictured the baby to be a shock but would remember the way their father randomly made hot, passionate love to me. I would chalk it up to God's timing and-

"-baby?"

I blinked, realizing I let my thoughts drift off while Johnathan was talking. I felt myself flush and apologized to my man for my lack of attention. He smirked.

"What you thinkin' about?"

I flushed. "Don't worry about it. What were you saying?"

"Hm. I was only saying I needed to make this shit work because you're a part of my life now and those Chanel bags ain't cheap."

I giggled, waving him off. "You're going to make it work because that's who you are. Besides, I don't need Chanel bags. I can't picture walking around with a bag that costs that much money on a regular basis."

"Because you're more of a Gucci girl."

"Maybe. But still."

I stood up, deciding to walk over to my man. He pulled his chair out to make room for me as I straddled him. He wasted no time in closing his arms around me and leaning in to kiss my lips.

"Don't feel like you have to spend outrageous amounts of money on me to keep me happy, baby. I'm not the high fashion girl that needs a closet full of runway clothes. I love Jays. I love Timbs."

"I know. I like that about you. I was just saying, you never know what you're going to like in the future. You might want to retire your Jays for some Louboutin's. I know once Shaunte starts getting into your head about certain shit, you'll decide she's right. Either way, let's stop acting like you don't like certain luxuries."

I giggled, nodding as I leaned in to kiss him one more time. I tasted the syrup on his tongue and melted as I kissed him all over again.

"I thought you wanted me to eat breakfast?"

I giggled as Johnathan pushed his plate aside, reaching up to rest his hand on the back of my neck. His thumb massaged my jaw as he looked into my eyes.

"I do. You just put me in a mood when you talk about taking care of me."

"I get it. Smelling this food while I was sleep knowing I wasn't down there cooking it made my dick hard earlier. You sure you don't want to move in?"

"Hm. You expecting me in a maid uniform? Cleaning your house? Doing your laundry? Washing the dishes?"

Johnathan chuckled. "I don't like the uniform. Just wear the apron so I can get a view of that juicy ass at all times."

I giggled. "So fuckin' mannish."

"Nah, that's what you get," he said, kissing down my neck. "You being smart and I'm just putting it out there. You think I don't already want you here?"

"I know you do."

He patted me on my backside. "I'm not in want of a maid. I want you. I want you to be comfortable. I want this. All the other stuff is extra."

"Extra, huh? So basic shit like doing the laundry and making sure the house doesn't look like shit is extra?"

Johnathan nodded. "In the future I want this to be our home. You cook, I clean. You do the laundry; I'll make sure some other shit is right. I don't want you feeling like you have to run a whole house by yourself and I'm just sitting around scratching my balls just because I made a few dollars and I assume you're home just looking pretty. We're not most couples...so expecting certain treatment is crazy."

"Besides...I want you to cook for me because you love me. Send my suits to the tailor because you love me. Have my lunch prepped because you love me. Maybe you pull up on me at a showing with a trench coat on and nothing else because you couldn't wait for me to get home..."

I leaned in, my lips dangerously close to his. "Because I want you and nobody else can do it for me."

He groaned, pressing his lips against mine. We kissed each other until the rest of our food ran cold. I was surprised that he hadn't pressed for more action but melted in his arms anyway as we kissed. I felt every bit of his love in his kisses. I felt my heart filling up with the way his hands possessively sat on my waist.

My heart was open to all of it anyway just because I felt his love. It was the inspiration. I knew I made cheeky comments, but I also knew that I wouldn't mind in the slightest just because he showed me that he loved me. In only a couple of days, my new man made me feel things my previous man hadn't. However, Johnathan was focused on the future, and I was focused on the present.

"I love you, Johnathan."

I pulled away long enough to say that. I hadn't realized I was crying until he reached up and wiped the tears from my face. I leaned into his touch.

"Why you crying, baby?"

"I don't know. I guess I'm happy. You really loved me and I..."

"Should've just got with me?" his brow raised. "Yeah but I'm not mad at you. I'm mad at myself. Could've been had your pretty ass with me."

"Stop being mad at yourself. We're here now."

"We are. I'm about to make up for lost time, too."

I giggled as he stood up and made the walk from the kitchen to the bedroom. I giggled, until I caught sight of our dishes now littering the table.

"Baby the dishes-"

"-I'll get them later. I want my snack now."

I wasn't going to complain about that. Besides, I was quickly becoming addicted to my boyfriend's brand of loving and knew I wasn't going to recover from it any time soon. I was lost in him already and the fact of the matter was I was afraid. I wasn't afraid of him per se but most happy times for me didn't last. At some point or the other something comes along to take it away.

I was in the deepest throes of love with Johnathan. So much that I knew if he decided to walk away from me, I would be devastated. I would lose twice instead of once. Losing the best friend I had in him was a struggle but losing the lover? I knew after him, another man couldn't fill his shoes.

So, we had to make it. There was no turning back.

Johnathan Barnes

The next two days were dedicated to moving Kiara's things out of her place with Julien. I hadn't gone in person just to keep the peace, but Uriel and Lashawn had gone in my stead. For some reason, Julien was quiet around the presence of my friend. I knew had I gone it wouldn't have ended well...at least that was the feeling I'd gotten from the last time. I wasn't trying to spend any time in Central Booking behind Julien's nonsense, so I deigned to stay away. My energies were better put to use hiring a lawyer for my love.

Julien kicking her out of the house meant that he had to come up with some sort of deal to compensate her. I knew he wasn't ready to sell but I knew he was planning something underhanded by forcing her to vacate. Still, I knew she helped him buy the house and if he tried anything it was going to cost him in the long run should she find her name missing from the deed.

That'd been on my plate and then studying for my Broker's exam was on the agenda for most of the day. I hadn't taken any breaks until Kiara texted me by evening:

Bae: I miss you. How's studying?

Me: It's going. Everything's packed away?

Bae: Everything's packed away. Uriel and Lashawn were a huge help.

Me: Okay good.

Bae: L says you should slide through he and Shawn's crib. They want to play spades.

I rolled my eyes. I wasn't truly in the mood to play spades more than I wanted to lay up with my woman and make love to her again. I thought about the last round I had before she left for the day, and I felt I needed that one more time. Being that she was still camping out with me for a little while though, I knew it was bound to happen.

I asked her if Lashawn cooked because in my mind it didn't make sense to go if she hadn't done so. I wasn't going to brave rounds of playing spades with the most disrespectful players in the world on an empty belly. It just didn't make sense.

Bae: She's suggesting Wing Stop on you and L's dime LMAO

I again rolled my eyes but decided it was better than nothing. Besides, I hadn't hung out with Uriel in a few weeks.

Me: I guess baby. I'll swing by in a few.

Bae: I'm waiting for you.

I smiled, thinking about how much deeper her words hit now that we were together. I wanted to send a more suggestive text but decided to behave and ended my study session. I grabbed my keys, wallet, and phone before heading out the door, making sure to lock it in the process.

I hopped in my car and drove the distance to my friend's house, which was about forty minutes from where I was at. Traffic hadn't been unforgiving, so it hadn't taken long. The scenery changed as I drove from Bed-Stuy to Starrett City. It took me about twenty minutes to find a parking space but once I had, I unapologetically slid in. Another driver hopefully asked me if I were leaving, and I was all too happy to dash his dreams and hope he had decent luck finding a space. My car would stand there until I was ready.

Delmar Loop had been renovated recently and so the area appeared to be lush with its green, rolling hills and open basketball courts. Little kids made themselves at home at the humble park, reminding me of a time when life was simpler.

I walked to Uriel and Lashawn's building, pressed the corresponding button for their apartment and waited a few seconds before I was buzzed in.

A short elevator ride upwards led me to their door where I knocked on it. Kiara answered the door, and I took my lady in with a smile. Her almond eyes brightened as her eyes met mine. Her full, glossy lips pulled into a helpless smile, and she rushed into my arms. I chuckled lightly, pulling her hair back gently and taking a kiss.

"Johnny..."

"Uh-uh! Not making out in my house!"

I blinked, forgetting we weren't at my house. I chuckled, releasing Kiara to close the door. Lashawn and Uriel stood next to each other, twin grins on their faces.

"About got damn time," Uriel said. "Now I can stop watching y'all act fuckin' stupid."

I chuckled. "Easy, man. Easy."

Uriel sucked his teeth. "Let me go get these fuckin' cards, man. This relationship shit new but me and Lashawn whippin' y'all ass ain't!"

I waved him off. "Man, first of all, you cappin' because you and Lashawn barely bustin' grapes out here."

I turned to Kiara, taking her hand and lightly pulling her towards the dining room table. Lashawn was already grinning, cat-like and I just shook my head. I knew they'd been trash talking about us for a while now, but I wasn't fazed. We'd been a long time coming and out of all my friends that I vented to, Uriel was the one I'd choose out of the three. I knew Shaunte was more of Kiara's speed but seeing Lashawn's reaction already let me know she'd been waiting on the sidelines with Uriel for something to happen.

Now we were going to play spades like it always was this way.

We played amicably until Kiara and I caught a bad hand. Suddenly Uriel and Lashawn were the best players in the history of playing spades, ever. I winked at my girl from my position, catching her looking dismayed because we were getting beat and I watched her blush. This time it was the luck of the draw rather than either of us playing terribly.

"Y'all might as well bet a blind seven or blind eight," Lashawn quipped, dealing out the next hand. "Y'all ain't beating us but at least you won't go down bad."

"We still might go down worse if we listen to that advice. Let's see what we get, baby," Kiara answered back, rolling her eyes.

I smirked, "It might not be the worst idea. We might have seven books."

Kiara frowned her face thoughtfully. "Hm. If you think we can pull it off, let's do it."

Uriel chuckled lightly but kept his thoughts to himself, for once. Uriel was generally humble in most instances, but spades wasn't a sport he was quiet on. I wondered if he and his girl were just equipped to pick and choose when to pick and prod their opponents.

I almost decided against the blind seven but shook my head and told Kiara we'd do it. She smirked as she picked up her hand. I watched her face go flat and felt my stomach drop. Still, I looked at my hand and was pretty pleased with how it was shaking up. Looking into my love's face I shrugged, half-heartedly and swallowed a chuckle as Uriel's face hardened.

"Y'all talk across the board again and that'll be three books, nigga."

"Calm your tits, ain't nobody talkin'."

"Oh, so her face falling and you looking sad ain't talking?" Lashawn said. "Please, John. Nobody got time for y'all today."

Kiara giggled. "Nobody's talking. Nobody's signaling. If y'all so lit why you actin' scared?"

"Don't do that. The rules are the rules," Uriel shrugged.

"Y'all just in our business," I said. "Let's go."

With that said, we went through the hands. It looked shaky at first but by the fourth hand I started understanding why Uriel was kicking up dust. Although he and Lashawn had bid seven books themselves, they weren't going to make seven.

Kiara and I on the other hand should've taken Lashawn's snarky suggestion to make eight. The aforementioned did sarcastically say that once we went through every hand. It caused Kiara and I to laugh and Lashawn still hopped up to twerk.

"We still beat y'all asses, though!"

Kiara rolled her eyes but looked over at me with a smile. I found myself smiling back as she walked over to me and made herself home in my lap. I squeezed her lightly.

"A win is a win."

I nodded, deciding her summation of the game was right and I was riding with it. Uriel shrugged.

"Nah, nigga. Y'all lost. Don't try to make it romantic now."

I got weak with laughter but tapped my woman on the backside lightly.

"I'm ready to go, baby," I announced. "They ain't even order the wings."

"Nah, stay!" Lashawn said, cackling. "I can still order some wings."

"And listen to y'all gloat for another hour and a half? Nah, we good," I said, chuckling. "Plus, I gotta get back to studying."

"Yeah, right, nigga. Lie to somebody else."

Kiara busted out laughing, even as I took her hand and led her slowly to the door.

"Mind your business, L! He's been studying!"

"Studying anatomy, not real estate," Lashawn quipped, laughing at her own joke. "You helping him with those study sessions faithfully, huh, Key?"

Kiara flipped her off, but let my hand go to give her a hug. Lashawn returned the hug lovingly. She then hugged Uriel, one armed.

"Thanks, y'all. For today. I'm glad y'all were there."

Uriel nodded his head, his face frowned up. "Oh, definitely. I admit to only coming around because I wanted that nigga to say something sideways. He didn't have nothing for your boy, though."

I laughed, reaching over to give my man a pound and a one-armed hug. We looked at each other, already knowing what time it was. I was glad to hear things went smoothly without incident. Now my love could move on in peace.

At least, that's what the plan had been.

"Let us know when y'all reach home, though," Lashawn said. "And don't study too hard, Johnathan. You gotta let Key get some rest in between sessions."

Lashawn winked at us, and Kiara let a giggle slip that she hadn't been ready to and walked away, a blush on her face. I followed behind her as Lashawn closed the door behind us, grabbing my woman's hand and leading her to the elevator.

"I don't even talk about sexing you," Kiara giggled. "She needs to stop."

"You don't have to. It's all over you that I'm working that ass out."

"Johnny, stop."

I had pulled her into me and took another kiss from her lips, biting the bottom one. She lightly moaned for me and smiled.

"You really trying to study, baby?" she asked, softly.

I reached down to grab a handful of her backside and chuckled, leaning to kiss her once more. The elevator dinged and I let her go, taking her hand in mine again. We entered, me absentmindedly rubbing the top of her hand while I pressed for the main level.

"Of course not. Studying was done when you texted me earlier today. I'm ready to tear that pretty ass up."

Kiara flushed, and I chuckled.

"What's wrong, baby? I'm tiring you out?"

"No. I'm excited."

She leaned into me, and I wrapped an arm around her waist, drawing her near. I almost wanted to sigh at how soft she was in my arms. I wanted to kiss on her some more but remembered we really were in public and decided against it. I'd have enough time when we reached home.

I thought of the word home and was slightly saddened, knowing she'll be ready to move out as soon as she found her own space. I'd gotten too used to her being around already but knew I couldn't look at it as the end but rather a preview. I hadn't thoroughly thought things through when I approached the love of my life. I had but at the same time, she was drawing lines in the sand, and I would still have to earn her and then keep earning her.

Still, she was worth it, and I wanted every action of mine to prove that.

Chapter Six

Kiara David

Moving was a huge chore. A few days with Johnathan were turning into weeks. I was nearing two months at the point I was at, and it was becoming harder to gain the motivation to move out. Still, I knew I needed to. As much as I wanted to lay up under Johnathan every day, I needed the time alone. I needed to wake up to my own space. I wanted to wake up in my own bed. I wanted to just take the time to enjoy my own company. I never did it before as much of my life was dedicated to Julien.

I loved Julien. I made love to Julien. I went out of my way for Julien. The period in his life in which he didn't realize his football dreams took a huge toll on me, though at the time, I was willing to love him through his struggles. I thought at the end of that road, I'd have been rewarded with a deeper level of commitment-a ring to say the least-but nothing ever came. Suddenly, his nights at the office started being longer and his temperament with me much shorter. Before long, I'd be crying to Johnathan because the careless cheating started all over again. Lipstick smudges on his collar would be found on wash day. Perfume that wasn't mine would permeate off his body when he leaned in to greet me on days when his mood was jovial.

It was a conundrum to me. Instead of him confessing to me that I wasn't the one for him and letting me go, he kept holding on and seeing women outside of our relationship. Instead of me walking away, I heard his apologies and stayed. Familiarity bred fear of seeing what was on the other side.

The change with Johnathan came way too fast and as overjoyed as I was to be with him, I needed to slow down. I was hopeful that my boyfriend understood my needs and wants. Moving in together at this stage was risky. Plus, I wanted all the things with Johnathan that had been lacking at least upwards of five years with Julien.

I wanted all kinds of dates. I wanted the kind of dates where we got to know each other. I knew there was still more to Johnathan that I didn't know, even after all this time. I knew there were things about me that he had yet to figure out. I wanted fun dates. I wanted coffee dates. I want him to pop up on me with flowers and wine. I want the surprise, romantic dinner dates that happen after I've had a hard day at work. I wanted it all and I wanted it with him.

I want to spend weekends with him at his place and vice versa. I want us to experience it all and I feel the only other logical step after I move in with him is to get married. I'd already made that mistake years ago. Julien had a live-in wife without the ring. I'd been supplying everything for free, so he hadn't had to make a date with the jeweler.

Those were my thoughts as I opened Instagram and realized I hadn't had the foresight to unfollow my ex.

I'd opened the app out of boredom while Shaunte and I did some furniture shopping for my new place. I had just settled on my living room couch and was excited. We'd been waiting for the salesman to come back with other pertinent information when I pulled out my phone. I quietly scoffed at the picture and tapped Shaunte, who'd been on her phone.

"What's up?"

I shoved my phone into her face and watched my friend raise a brow and then chuckle at the caption:

When one door closes, the other one opens. To my future wife, I love you, endlessly.

"This nigga is a true narcissist," Shaunte scoffed. "Unfollow and block him, immediately. Make sure you don't like the picture either, Key."

I giggled. "I'm not that down bad."

"Sometimes women act like they have something to prove to a nigga after they've moved on. I don't want you to feed his ego in any way, shape, or form. You've moved on and are making moves for yourself, so I don't want this moment to make you relapse."

"It won't be a relapse. It's more of a...reinforced lesson," I sighed. "Johnathan told me he wouldn't mind if I moved in with him but I...just can't."

Shaunte nodded. "You shouldn't. Not this early. I...feel I made the same mistake and now I'm paying for it."

I frowned. "What do you mean?"

Shaunte gave me a sad smile. "I haven't told anybody this yet but...I left Micah right after your birthday party."

The world as I knew it stopped turning. I gasped, my shock stilling me. I was surprised, mostly because Shaunte and Micah had been through it all together. They were each other's friends. They were each other's first boyfriend and girlfriend. Each other's first times. I thought they'd be the fairy tale relationship I believed in, and that Micah would get on bended knee for my friend. I was sure of many of those things, so the news felt like a freezing gallon of cold water was thrown at me.

"Left, Shaunte? Why?"

"Well...when you're with someone as long as I've been with Micah or even with you and Julien, you know your mate. You can deny the rhythms as much as you want but in the long run you know the deal. I...realize that I'm not Micah's end game. Maybe once upon a time I was. But now? No, I'm not. Or at the very least, he wants to explore other women."

"So...you let him go? How are you feeling? Why didn't you tell me before now?"

"Because you're happy, Kiara. You're finally happy and you don't need me dumping on you every two minutes because I'm sad."

"I get it but...two things can be true at once. I don't have to stop my happiness by giving you a listening ear, Tay. We've been friends too long for this, come on now."

I pulled my friend in a hug in the middle of the furniture department and rubbed her back. She didn't cry but I could feel her sadness as she shared that bit of news with me.

"Thanks, Key." She sighed."But still, I just want you to learn from...our mistake."

I giggled. "What am I learning here?"

"Keep yourself expensive and exclusive and make a nigga work for it. I think right when we moved in together...I stopped making him work for it. Now...he's ready for a new mountain to conquer."

"But...why not put yourself in a position to be conquered again?" I questioned. "You could just-"

"-start the process over? Maybe. I'm not counting us out, totally. I just know, right now as it stands, I'm unhappy with our relationship. Plus, I see him, and I know him. He needs to get over whatever phase this is. And if it's not a phase, I need to be positioning myself for a man who will do the work and always want to do the work. Any real woman still has to have a sense of self. Most other women would tell you to make your life easier and move in with John. While John is a good man...sis, he's still a man. Make him sweat. If he loves you, he'll do the work."

I nodded and then proceeded to do what my friend told me without argument. There was no reason for me to keep following Julien on social media anyway. I should have unfollowed him some time ago, but I didn't want rumors and snide remarks to follow me wherever we went. Most of his friends and family hadn't liked me but that was because they pictured him with another type of woman.

They finally got their wish and so did he. Now, I genuinely hoped he was happy. It was time for me to be happy as well.

Johnathan Barnes

Micah was in a foul mood after delivering the news to us that Shaunte left him. I, for one, was in shock because I fully expected an engagement announcement this year. I wondered to myself what inspired the breakup but wasn't sure that I wanted to ask.

"Said some dumb shit about knowing me and knowing I'm not fully with her," he shrugged. "I don't get her, man."

Xander chuckled dryly, as he sipped from the Corona Uriel had passed him earlier. Uriel deigned to do the same thing and we both looked at each other, unsure of how to approach the news he'd dropped on us.

"Y'all niggas can act like y'all feel sorry for a nigga."

"I don't," Xander deadpanned. "You single, Lil' Wayne. Go meet some new bitches."

I chuckled, unsure of how to respond to that. Micah's expression hardened, and I almost thought a fight would break out. Uriel sucked his teeth at Xander's response, opening his mouth when Micah shrugged his shoulders.

"You're right."

My jaw slackened, surprised at his answer. I for sure thought Micah would say something different but he hadn't. Somehow, Xander's answer was satisfactory but it wasn't making sense to me. If he wanted to prove to Shaunte that he was with her, truly with her, why was his next move heading out to the club to meet new women?

I was at a loss for words when Micah searched his phone for a club and Xander made a few suggestions off the top of his head. He and Micah ran the play as if they were getting ready to hit the field and it left both me and Uriel thrown for a loop. I could tell by the look on Uriel's face.

"Nigga, the fuck are you talkin' about? You're nearing your mid-thirties telling another grown ass man to get into new pussy like he don't already have pussy waiting on his ass?"

Xander shrugged at Uriel. "Not everybody gets to come home to Lashawn. Not everybody gets to dig out the girl of their dreams. And apparently, the Shaunte's of the world don't wanna be kept. So, what's next for a nigga? Cry to us like a bitch? Nah, he needs to see what's out there."

"Or he proves to the love of his life that he's with her," Uriel pressed, "Nah, Mike, don't listen to this shit."

Micah looked up at Uriel and shook his head.

"Xan is right, though," Micah said. "She had me damn near begging the other night for her to stay. She wouldn't. I been with her too long to have to go through changes with her."

"You also been down too long to not have been thinking about marriage," I said. "Respectfully. What else is supposed to be the next step?"

"When I'm ready, nigga," Micah shrugged. "Besides, she's acting like she doesn't wanna meet a nigga at the end of the aisle so what do I do with that?"

"It's not rocket science, Mike," Uriel said. "Find a fucking ring, get down on bended knee and tell her what's up. That's probably what has her upset. Still, you don't know until you figure out where she's at and run down on her for some answers."

Micah shook his head, "Nah, I'm good on her for now."

Uriel and I shared another look and Xander laughed.

"Anyway, like I said, let's get right and run out."

Xander stood up, stretching out and laughed at both me and Uriel again, shrugging his shoulders.

"Look, y'all got solid situations. Micah doesn't. I love Tay but if she on bullshit she on bullshit. Same across the board for Key and Shawn. No use in giving your strength to a woman who doesn't want to be kept."

Uriel opened his mouth and then closed it. I lost each and every thought that might have knocked sense into Micah when I saw he was actually taking Xander's advice.

"You think you want to be out there and you don't, nigga," Uriel said. "You better make up with Tay and make some shit happen. Take it from homeboy talking to Steph Curry's father."

Xander busted out laughing. I joined in when I remembered the Twitter thread warning the older gentleman to make it work with his wife.

"Fuck outta here, don't try to scare my nigga back. I have a wingman now."

"No, shit," I said, chuckling. "You need to get your ass right, too. You not tired, nigga?"

"The day you tired of fucking Kiara is the day I'm tired of running through bitches," Xander shot back at me.

"Besides, who the fuck are you to talk to me, Johnny-Boy?! You were the man a few years ago!"

I ran a hand down my face. It was true that I had a rotation going a few years ago but it was respectable. I had a few women that I kept up with but kept things light. I had fun in college. Same with all my boys. We met girls who wanted to have fun and we kept it fun for the most part. Xander was the one who tried for a relationship back at Clark, but things had gone south with the lady. She'd been trying to get back and Xander had been stringing her along ever since. Unsure of who was more wrong in the situation most days.

The other thing about me, however, was that I knew that I always wanted Kiara. The ones I tried to have more with either caught up on the game or I had to put a break to things before someone got hurt. Most times I came to the realization that I was just using the person to get over my hurt of the situation. I had more women walk away from me than anybody realized. Maybe except Uriel.

"I did alright," I shrugged. "But we all knew what it was. I knew where my heart was at, but I had my fun."

"You did so don't tell this nigga he can't have fun while Shaunte figuring some shit out. That's all I'm saying."

"You just want a wingman," Uriel started laughing. "Save that bullshit you talkin'. It's like this though, Mike. You either try to make the shit work or have fun. Just understand the stakes. Just like you single, Lil' Wayne, Beyonce a single lady, too. She meets a next nigga who putting in the work and you can forget it. Just a fair warning."

"Worry your pretty head about Lashawn," Micah said. "I'm good over here."

Uriel tossed me one more look and I shrugged my shoulders. Micah was grown and had it figured out already. I wasn't going to be the one to beg him to do what he knows he needs to do.

"I'm breaking out," I announced, standing up.

"This nigga stood up like he getting ready to take over the world. Knowing all he's going to do is see Kiara."

I shrugged, chuckling incredulously. Same difference in my opinion. Kiara literally was my world so yeah; I was ready to take it over. Stake my claim all over again. Stake my flag on her moon.

Besides, she'd been texting the bat signal, so I had to comply. Sitting around listening to Micah get ready to ruin his life wasn't my idea of a good time. Not when for years, he was the envy of the crew in my opinion. He'd gotten with his best friend early on. He'd gone through every single step in life with her. I wished I hadn't been foolish. The fun Xander spoke on? I didn't even truly want that. I would've clipped every single one of those girls had Kiara said so. That was how much I wanted her.

Thinking of Xander's comment, I almost wanted to comment that he was jealous that he couldn't do the same but knew that'd incite a rant I didn't want to hear. Sometimes wisdom was knowing when to keep your mouth shut.

"Y'all have fun now."

"You have fun with your one and we're gonna have fun with our five or six," Xander shrugged, laughing. "I love the bitches and they love me. No point in settling when I can have them all."

I chuckled lightly, deciding not to comment. Again, my one was my world. I needed the time with her anyway since she was moving out soon. She was in the process of looking at apartments with a realtor friend of mine. I tagged along, mostly for support. She was narrowing her choices down to three spaces she'd seen that she fell in love with. I was pretty certain she might move to this space near me. It wasn't next door, but it wasn't up the block either. It was a luxury space in Bushwick that I saw in her eyes she liked the most. I was still slightly chagrined with the fact that she was moving but I knew she needed the time.

Our relationship happened randomly and the break from Julien happened randomly. It was a fallout that I hadn't thought about as much as I should have before making us happen. Still, we were together and that was all that mattered to me.

As for my friend, I hoped he knew what he was doing.

Chapter Seven

Kiara David

Two Months Later...

"Johnny, please..."

My boyfriend's laughter was lazy as I stood on tip-toes and kissed him along his face. I was currently begging him to shop with me at Target so I could start picking some things up to decorate my place for Christmas. So far, he wasn't with it.

"You know I hate going with you to Target. Might as well be taking you to LV or something."

"Oh, so you'd rather take me anywhere else except Target?"

Johnathan chuckled, running his hands through my hair. He pulled my face back to take a kiss from me and I knew I had him.

"You do the most at Target." he said, "Aren't you supposed to be boycotting?"

I giggled, "I don't have a dog in that fight and besides, if they're not shopping at Target, then that means more space and time for me to find what I want."

Johnathan chuckled, tipping my face to meet his face, "You hell, sometimes, girl."

I shrugged. While I understood the uproar behind Target making their decision to end DEI programs, I don't believe our brothers and sisters were benefitting from them as much as they thought they were. I'd rather they did away with the program instead of trying to save face when it only supported a select group. With that being said, there were more pressing things in the country going on than Target's DEI stance.

"I'm only going for a few things, Johnny."

I looked up at him through my lashes and he smirked, grabbing a handful of my backside as he leaned in, kissing my lips again. I had caught him rifling through my kitchen cabinets for a snack not too long ago. Suddenly, I became his snack when I stepped into his space and posed the question.

"You always say that shit, Key, and we're in there for a solid three hours because you just have to look at everything, just in case."

He said the last part in a high pitched mockery of my voice, and I started giggling.

"I make it worth your while, don't I?"

"You gonna make it worth my while this time, too."

He caged me in between his body and my island and I shivered as he leaned in and kissed me once more. I moaned as his kisses moved to my neck and he lightly bit my shoulder. I almost changed my mind about my shopping trip when he pulled back, looking into my eyes.

"Let's go with your spoiled ass," he mumbled, licking his lips.

If I weren't so horny in that moment I would've squealed in happiness. As it were, I swallowed, moving around my apartment to gather my things. I slowly pulled my mind out of the fog Johnathan created with a smile on my face.

My apartment was lovely to me. It wasn't the grandiose settings I was used to with Julien, or the stately, romantic feel of Johnathan's brownstone. However, it was my own little box that I could call home. I say box because it's New York City. What's the greatest city in the world without overinflated prices for much less than you pay for?

Still, my apartment was lovely. My kitchen had white and blue cabinetry with a fun, colorful backsplash. My appliances were the ever-present stainless steel that made every apartment 'luxury'. I had to buy my own island because one wasn't present and I needed it when I cooked. I paid for a two bedroom so I could keep my workspace separate from my living space. I liked to call it my 'cloffice', because all of my extra clothes could be stored there but I could still have a functional desk and workspace in the mix. My actual bedroom was chic. A queen-sized bed was my comfort at the end of most trying days. I haven't had many yet but the ones I had made me grateful to be able to sink into my bed in peace.

There was nobody on my back about why dinner wasn't done. Nobody to question my movements for the day 'when I was home all day'. It was absolute freedom that I hadn't known I needed until the opportunity arose.

That's what made me most grateful for my best-friend-turned-boyfriend. I believe whether I ended up with him or not, leaving Julien was definitely the aim. I hadn't realized how deep my trauma was because I was with him daily. Now that I was away from him, I could breathe.

Two months later and I had to admit, I felt light years ahead.

We walked out of my apartment, hand-in-hand and hopped in Johnathan's car again. I laughed at the fake annoyed look he had on his face and swallowed my giggles as he turned an eye at me. His face softened as he took in my happiness.

"You really be happy over the small things," he said, stroking my chin. "You're adorable."

"Hm. So you're suddenly happy to be taking me?"

"You're smiling because I said yeah. So...yeah," he shrugged, turning his face away.

I smirked, catching him blush and felt my heart almost implode on itself. I hadn't known that the right relationship would be easy to enjoy. After a time, I was under the belief that love was supposed to hurt.

With Johnathan I learned that it wasn't. Not one bit. Not the way they painted for us girls growing up. Between my parents that didn't end well, to other family members who got it wrong, I was happy to be one who finally got it right. Even if Johnathan and I didn't work out, I now had a standard. I can't let a man love me any old kind of way. I have an example of how it's supposed to go.

I intertwined my fingers with Johnathan's as we drove and sighed as he caressed the top of my hand with his thumb. Another smile was on my face while Snoh Allegra played softly in our background. It was the prerequisite of a beautiful afternoon and a lovely evening.

"Thank you, baby."

Johnathan slowed down at a light and smirked. He lifted our hands and kissed mine, lingering on my skin for a second.

"My pleasure, baby."

Johnathan Barnes

It was an almost routine trip to Target. I was annoyed with the motions, but it made my lady happy, so I was happy to make do with whatever she wanted. I noticed this trip was quite a bit shorter, mostly because she knew she was only after Christmas decorations. I didn't complain, mostly because I knew she was making the effort not to drag me down every single aisle. Since our visit didn't take as much time as normal, I slid her some money and told her to get Starbucks on me. Her squeal of happiness made me chuckle. I tapped her backside as she skipped away from her cart. I watched her, bouncing with happiness.

I'd been so into her that when someone cleared their throat I jumped slightly and turned around. I took in the lady in front of me, trying to figure out if I knew her at all. She was attractive but all I felt was annoyance that she tore my attention away from my love.

"Can I help you?"

"You don't remember me, Johnathan?"

The woman crossed her arms, partly bringing my attention to her breasts. I knew she'd done it on purpose so I raised my head back up to her face so I could figure who she had to be. She knew my name, so something had to give.

"I'm sorry to say I don't."

"Keisha!" she said. "We dated briefly back at Clark."

Her face came together and recognition hit hard. Then I remembered why our dating history was brief.

"How you been?" she asked, grinning. "I see you haven't changed much. Still fine."

Keisha took me in unabashedly and it caused me to chuckle, my discomfort starting to kick up a few notches. Single me would've humbly thanked her for her praise. Relationship me didn't want Kiara to overhear the interaction and think it was more than what it was.

"Appreciate that," I said. "How you been? You ever get married? Have kids?"

She rolled her eyes. "No and yes. I just had my son with Jared, but he decided to move on with someone else."

"Sorry to hear that, sis," I said. "I hope things turn around for you."

"Hm. They need to turn around with you."

I opened and closed my mouth at her audacity. I was trying to be polite, but she was forcing the issue. If she were looking for a savior, it wouldn't be me.

Someone yelled Kiara's name for her order. I turned back to see my woman walking to the barista and grabbing her drink.

"Hm. If I knew she was still in the picture I would've kept on walking. All the baddest was after you and that's what you chose?"

I bit down on my quick anger, not wanting to disrespect a sister in public over mine in an obvious way. Still, she did deserve correction. It was obvious to anyone back then as much as it was now.

"It's not the ones after me, it's the one I'm after," I shrugged. "Like I said, sis, I hope things turn around for you."

Keisha rolled her eyes and made her exit as Kiara walked up to me, her eyes curious. She looked so adorable and innocent that I leaned in, kissing the top of her head.

"Was that Keisha?" she asked, with a brow raised. "That's interesting."

"Yeah. Talking about a bunch of nothing," I said. "You ready to go?"

Kiara edged a look in the direction that Keisha walked away from in a huff. I saw my lady smile, putting together the conversation for herself before she looked up in my eyes and released a soft giggle. I shook my head at the pettiness as she walked on with her Starbucks, leaving me to push her cart outside.

We walked amicably toward my car and I loaded up her items in the car while she watched.

"You're really just going to stand there and watch?"

"Yes," she grinned. "Because you're fine and you're mine and I can."

"Stop acting like I put the earth back on its axis. I did what I was supposed to do."

"I didn't say-"

"You don't have to. I know you're pleased I sent her on her way but still, baby, that's regular."

"I still can watch you though because I can," she said, smirking. "And she's mad that she can't."

I smirked, loading in the last of her bags before slamming the trunk closed. I pulled my woman close to me, lifting her head up and kissing along her jaw. I reached her ear, biting the tip and enjoying her quick shudder.

"Stop being petty. Everybody knew I was yours, except you. You just realizing that."

"And I can enjoy the realization," Kiara said, looking up at me. "Take me home so I can enjoy the realization some more, Johnny."

I smirked as she pulled away from me, walking to the other side of the car. I walked behind her, stopping her short of grabbing the door handle. I opened it, watching my love lower herself into the seat before slamming the door.

I walked back to the other side, pulling the door open and lowering myself in the seat. I started the car and proceeded to head out.

The ride back to her house wasn't long. I drove one handed on the wheel while the other held her hand in mine. More love songs played in the background and I sighed, enjoying myself.

Pulling up to her home, we gathered her things and carried them back to her apartment. Kiara directed me to place her bags in the living area as she closed and locked her door. She asked me if I wanted anything as I made myself comfortable and I declined, not really wanting much but her in my arms.

It warmed me that she wanted the same. After she drank a glass of water, she walked over to me on the couch, straddling me and leaning in once more to kiss my lips. My hands found their home on both sides of her waist, looking at her as she pulled away.

"Thanks for taking me, Johnny," she said, grinning. "I love you."

"It was nothing, baby."

I pulled her back into me, taking another kiss from her lips. Over and over again we kissed. Sometimes soft, sometimes hard. Some moments she opened her mouth to grant me access to her tongue and others, I took the time to outline her lips with my tongue. The feel of her soft lips pulled me back in for more. When she pulled away, the only thing stopping me from pulling her back was the dopey smile that came across her face as she took me in. I grinned back, shocked that all we were doing was kissing. We kissed like we were making up for lost times we'd never taken advantage of. We were like teenagers in my girlfriend's apartment, kissing as if her parents would walk in any moment and catch us. We kissed without abandon. We kissed slowly, as if the moment would end without notice.

"I have a confession."

Her giggle was nervous and caused me to chuckle, wondering why my woman was feeling silly at the moment.

"What, baby?"

I playfully tapped her behind and watched the blush come across her face so beautifully. With a grin, I slapped it again, a little harder. She bit her bottom lip and told me to chill out. I felt myself harden as I saw her rising lust. Her slim but shapely body called to me as she sat on my lap looking like a piece of caramel candy that I was ready to devour. Still, my curiosity of her confession egged at me more.

"I remember seeing you kissing on Keisha years ago."

I was shocked that Keisha was still a subject matter when I couldn't even remember her face. From the little I remember, we shortly dated at Clark and I thought I'd be with her seriously. However, the more I got to know her, the more I felt we were better suited as friends. At the time she felt the same way or at least I thought so. Seeing her earlier made me realize she blamed Kiara for my stepping away. While Kiara hadn't been the first reason, she was the overall reason why I walked away from a few women I could've been with.

"When?" I questioned. "I didn't even fuck with her that long."

"I know. I just remembered walking out of class, and happened to catch you walking with her. Before y'all went y'all separate ways she walked up to you and kissed you. You kissed her back and I wanted to beat both y'all asses so bad."

The confession made me weak with laughter, shaking my head at how silly her being upset was. Still, she couldn't have been so sure of me because of moments like that. It was the biggest reason I didn't hold a grudge against her for not wanting to bet on me back then.

"That's not funny!"

"It's funny as fuck," I shrugged. "Because I would've rather been kissing you."

"Anyway, saying that to say, I was bitter because I never thought I'd ever get to kiss you. I always thought you were perfect for me. I daydreamed about us while I fought with Julien. There were days I thought about saying fuck it all and just confessing. But I was scared."

I ran a hand down my face, smirking at the jealousies I didn't know she'd been dealing with. I didn't truly stop to think about what my dating around could've been doing to her although she was dating Julien. Still, I didn't regret my movements. Life stopped for nobody.

"I'm glad you didn't," I replied. "It might not have gone well back then."

Kiara questioned why.

"I...would be remiss if I said that man never loved you. He did. His problem was he didn't let himself explore and date around before stepping to you. I halfway think the nigga knew I liked you and decided to press you first but again...baby, that was on me."

The memory never failed me. Xander had finally gotten me to confess that I had feelings for Kiara. Julien heard it somehow and being that we were already rivals, he ran with that information. Right at the end of high school, he stepped to her. Kiara is hyped because past us, Julien was the guy all the girls were after. I think he stepped to her to piss me off but then decided he wanted to keep her around. Before long, they were dating seriously and I was left to figure out how to get over someone that I wanted since freshman year of high school.

"Hm. So you really not mad at me? I was mad at me," she said, her voice soft. "I could've-"

"-yeah. You could've left him. But...everything for its reason, baby."

I meant that. It wasn't just something slick to say to put her heart at ease. I truly believe that things might've gone left for real had she left him too soon. I think it might've gotten too hectic if we were still in college.

I believe there were too many times when Julien should've just let her go and waited for the next episode with someone else. He was on the football team with Morehouse. He had his own run with women from the neighboring colleges. It would have made sense for him to cut Kiara loose, knowing he wasn't in the state of mind to be faithful.

I know he hadn't mostly because he was too afraid, she'd run straight to me if he had. I know I wouldn't have turned her away in a benevolent manner because they should work things out. I wouldn't have played that role, simply because I'd been wanting her. I think he would've gone off the deep end and neither of us would've graduated because at some point, a reckoning would've had to happen.

Because I wasn't letting her go.

Those thoughts were on my mind as I pulled her into me and kissed her lips once more. I grabbed the back of her neck, caressing the side with my thumb.

"I love kissing you."

Kiara's eyes lowered and I could tell my statement took the wind out of her sails.

It was the truth that every woman before her was a consolation prize. Well, once I realized and admitted that I had feelings for her. After that moment, I haven't remembered any of them. I could barely remember Keisha's presence in my life from years ago. In the wake of my love for Kiara, I couldn't give Keisha even a piece of my heart. The woman sitting on my lap effectively stopped any seed from growing in that kind of foundation.

If only she'd known back then. Still, I preferred the present.

"It's always been you, Key," I sighed. "Always."

On that admission, I leaned in, kissing her lips once more. The softness, the fullness, made me weak, even as I held her by the waist. When she pulled away and looked into my eyes, I smiled at her.

"Your petty ass," I chuckled, laughing harder when she hit me on the chest and slid off me.

"You hungry, baby?"

I watched as she went straight into the kitchen, grabbing something out of the fridge. I grunted, letting her know I was since I hadn't eaten before we left her house earlier. I smiled with glee and decided to turn on the TV so I wouldn't look like a creep just watching her the whole time.

Leaning back into her couch, I took in her space and smiled. I wanted her to move in with me eventually but that was my own selfishness talking. I realized she needed the time to enjoy her own surroundings and totally move on from Julien and the toxicity of that relationship. Still, some nights I could go for packing her whole place up and moving her in with me.

I enjoyed our togetherness. I always had. So, to have to leave her or watch her leave me hurt some days. Still, I understood that it was necessary. That was also after Shaunte explained it to me when I made a crass joke about not wanting to help my cause.

"If you want to keep her for real, you need to let her grow for a while in her own pot. When her roots outgrow the place, then you can repot her in your place. Calm your horny ass down."

It was advice I had to take on the chin, but I noted she was very right.

I also saw that it wasn't just the toxicity of Julien she had to grow out of but our overall situation that we'd been in for years. I felt Keisha was nobody but to Kiara she'd been a thorn in her side. One she was glad to watch me pull out of her.

Healing wasn't the linear process we all thought it to be. I couldn't talk much because I ached most days to knock on Julien's door and snuff him for any random occurrence I could remember. Our first go round wasn't enough in my opinion. Word on the street was that he was already engaged not even a month after he kicked my woman out of her home.

"Baby, we still seeing a lawyer about your house?"

The thought came unbidden in my mind. He truly kicked her out as if the house wasn't a house but an apartment. That part didn't make any sense to me.

"Oh, absolutely. I'm owed that."

Kiara said it calmly, but I knew the thought of what he'd done pissed her off to high heavens. I knew she wouldn't rest until she saw her money back for the stunt he pulled. I'd make sure it happened for her.

About twenty minutes later, she walked back into the living room with butter chicken and rice and the presentation caused me to raise a brow.

"Getting international with it?" I commented, taking my plate from her as she giggled a little bit,

"Just a little bit," she said. "I made this last night and it was so good! So, I figured I should share with you."

"Hm." I said, taking a bite, "It is good. Thank you, baby."

We ate companionably while watching Wildin' Out for the next few hours. We ate, drank, and cuddled until she fell asleep.

She woke up about an hour later and smiled apologetically at me. I chuckled and leaned in, kissing her lips.

"Why didn't you wake me back up?"

"Why you fall asleep on me?"

Kiara giggled as she stood up, stretching. I looked at her, licking my lips and standing up to join her after she reached her hand out to me. I let her lead me into her bedroom and stopped short as she stopped, turning around to kiss me on my lips.

"You want to join me in the shower?"

I smirked. "You know I do."

"You want to join me in my bed afterwards?"

"You didn't have to ask."

Kiara giggled and turned around. I gave her a pat on the backside for good measure. I thought about our day and decided it was a good one. I couldn't wait to have many more with her in the future.

I had a get-together at my place in lieu of a housewarming. It'd been a few months since I moved in so more than anything, I wanted a get together with the boys. What better time was there to have one than a Sunday evening. The only thing better was to have Kiara present. She'd been hesitant to come but I wasn't trying to hear her not being there. All of us watching the game included Kiara for the longest so I wasn't trying to have it be any different now.

Still, the welcome change of her using my kitchen to prep the snacks did something to me. She was moving efficiently but still doing a masterful job of deep frying two batches of buffalo wings and another set of lemon-pepper wings. I'd been sent to the store earlier to get the corresponding dips and beers that we'd enjoy later on.

I had prepped our drinks in big buckets of ice and situated them. I helped myself to one while I watched Kiara start to arrange the chicken wings on platters. Before she could start the next one I reached over to try to steal a piece when she popped my hand lightly.

"Go find something to do, Johnathan."

"I can't have a sample?" I grinned, "They look delicious."

"No!" she giggled, "It's bad enough you opened a beer but whatever. I have to finish this up so I can change."

Kiara had been wearing a navy blue form fitting two piece lounge set that was meant to help her cook more comfortably. It was basic and yet it did nothing but make me want to volunteer my services to help her out of it. I moved to her as she was still trying to make headway with arranging the wings and dips on the platters.

I walked up behind her, caging her in and leaning down to kiss the back of her neck. She moaned lightly, pausing her work and giggled as my arms wrapped around her.

"Baby, I have to finish..."

"I know. Just expressing my appreciation for you going through the trouble." I said, kissing her again, "Everything looks good, baby."

Kiara looked up at me with a smile that made me melt. Leaning back, she met me in the middle for a kiss on the lips and I pulled away as I saw her pleasured flush.

"You're welcome, baby." she said, "You have to get out now, though. I have to finish and now I don't want to."

I groaned at the implication but went with her wishes. We still had game night to host and I knew we could always pick up where we left off later on.

In the next hour, my pursuit of Kiara had been all but forgotten when the bell rang. I opened it to Xander and Micah. A boisterous display of laughter and dapping up ensued before we settled in the living room to catch the game. It was a few minutes before kick-off so I was blessed with the view of Kiara showing up comfortably dressed in a two piece lavender legging set. The top was loose-fitting and the leggings hugged those legs that I loved wrapped around me so much.

Uriel showed up not long after, apologizing for his lateness. I didn't say much, knowing that he got caught up with Lashawn as usual. The game hadn't been on long so he hadn't missed much.

Kiara was finishing up passing around our beers and told us to help ourselves with more later on. Once she showed everybody where the beer bucket was, she walked back into the kitchen. I was slightly embarrassed at how sad I was to watch her leave.

When she came back with her own Smirnoffs I watched as she tried to walk past me. I leaned forward, plucking her up by the waist and sat her on my lap. Immediately after, I could feel the stares from my boys.

"What?" I said, "We here to watch the game or watch me and mine?"

"You gotta relax." Xander chuckled, "We know that's you already. Let her breathe, nigga."

I laughed but let Kiara slide in the seat next to me, settling for wrapping an arm around her shoulder instead. The truth was, I just enjoyed having her close to me, more than staking my claim. I honestly just hadn't cared that the action would make everybody else uncomfortable.

Micah whistled as they cut to the cheerleaders, mentioning which ones he'd pick out of the line-up. Xander frowned thoughtfully at his choices, silently agreeing. I didn't have anything to add, especially with Kiara sitting up under me and Uriel hadn't added much to the conversation, either.

"None of them hold a candle to my girl, though, you trippin'."

Kiara had commented on their commentary, eyeing Micah with disgust. I was shocked at the look on her face and wondered if she'd heard news of their break up. I wasn't totally sure but by her reaction I was pretty certain she knew and that she was disappointed. I held disappointment for how he was moving as of late...we were supposed to be celebrating their engagement by now.

Micah spared Kiara a glance and said, "That might be true but this is just jokes. Relax."

I didn't know my body had gone stiff until Kiara reached down to squeeze my leg. I relaxed but grabbed her hand with my opposing one, pulling it up and kissing it. I gave her a knowing look and she smiled and winked at me. I thought our quick exchange had gone unnoticed until Uriel huffed.

"Ayo, we watching a game or nah?"

Kiara giggled and I threw up my hands in surrender. I could have mentioned that he and Lashawn were often much worse than Kiara and I but let it go. Kiara on the other hand decided not to.

"Look bro, we just chillin' like normal, like?"

She shuffled her hands for emphasis and Uriel joined in, mocking her, forcing laughter out of her.

"Nah, you're not just watching the game. You're making goo-goo eyes at ya boy and thinking we just gonna ignore it. Behave or get out."

She answered him with her middle finger and laid her head into my shoulder. A few more minutes went by without incident until Uriel's phone rang. He noted that Lashawn was calling him and let the call go to voicemail. Kiara questioned him on it. Uriel eyed her and then shook his head, silently asking her to let it go. Kiara went to retaliate to the silent demand and Uriel shook his head again.

"I promise we're fine, Mrs. Officer. No need to jump down my throat over your sis. She knows I'm watching the game, so I don't even know what she's calling about."

"You need to find out, then!"

Kiara's voice pitched. Uriel's eyes widened and she stared back, just as surprised by her own outburst. Taking a look around she noticed we all were looking at her, questioning her upset. She took a look at me and I looked back, wondering why Uriel ignoring Lashawn's call would get her so uptight in the first place.

It was suddenly uncomfortable for about thirty tense seconds.

"My bad, L," she said, her tone sheepish. "Forget that happened."

Uriel had shook off the look of betrayal on his face and understanding came over his face when Kiara stood up and leaned over to kiss me on the cheek. The look of confusion on my face had only deepened.

"I'm gonna hang out with Shaunte while y'all watch the game."

I wrapped my arm around her waist, holding her in place.

"Nah, baby for what? It's still chill, why you trying to leave?"

"This isn't my scene, bae. I'm good. I'll come back later."

My heart squeezed, although I saw the peace in her expression. I was lost on why she was getting ready to leave. It was the same as usual. I wasn't sure why things had to change when they were already fine as they were.

I thought about making that same point again but Kiara leaned in, kissing me fully on the lips. She took her time, kissing me once and then twice more with the promise that there was more when she returned to me. I heard the guys sucking their teeth at the display but I wanted to shoot the fair one with them first chance I had when my love walked out the door.

"I'll be back. Enjoy the game."

I tapped her behind as she turned to walk away.

"Y'all done chased my woman away." I grumbled, standing up to walk over to the beer bucket. Grabbing another one, I popped it up open and took a swig while I spied her Smirnoffs scattered inside. My heart squeezed a little bit, bewilderment of her departure sitting on my chest.

"You don't realize she's the opp now?" Uriel chuckled, "That's not our friend anymore, that's your girl."

My face hardened at Uriel's delivery, "What you mean? She's still Kiara! Y'all niggas trippin'."

"So, I can come over and clap Kiara's cheeks when I feel like it?"

Xander asked me the question with a smirk on his face and I saw red immediately.

"X, watch your fuckin' mouth."

"Nah, because that's the bullshit that we had to hear for years. Like L said, that's your girl." Xander pressed,

"So she's my girl now y'all on some new shit?"

"Yeah, I don't get what's so hard for you to comprehend, John." Uriel mentioned, "It's still love for her and all but her presence in your life is different now. She's not just our homegirl anymore, she's your woman. She can't really relate to us anymore at the level we were at. She's growing up."

I still wasn't totally understanding what that even meant. I said that much when Micah chuckled.

"She over here pressing us over the girls, John. That's not something she was doing years ago. She was our girl years ago. Down with the crew. Minus Shaunte the girls were our girls but not her friends. The girls are now her friends. She sympathizes with them now. She's watching me checking out other girls and defending Shaunte because it could be you doing the same thing to her. She watching L ignore Lashawn's call defending her because it could be you doing the same thing to her. She didn't realize it until she got on Uriel."

"She didn't say anything to me." Xander said, chuckling,

"She didn't have time to." Micah laughed, "She would've found a way, trust me."

"Nah, because I don't have commentary on other chicks like mine ain't bad and I wouldn't ignore her call if she called me right now. She wasn't wrong to say anything to y'all...she still the opp though, John. Just so you know."

I flipped them all off and we continued watching the game without further commentary on my girl and what changes she was going through. I wasn't totally sure that it was our relationship that was bringing about the changes. She was still my Kiara, only we were in a relationship. I got her every kiss and her every expression of love. I still didn't see how that totally translated to her and the boys dealing with her any differently than they were.

Uriel's explanation made sense but I just wasn't catching up. It seemed like I wouldn't until it was almost too late.

Chapter Eight

Kiara David

Quite a bit had changed between my last birthday and the one approaching. Johnathan had since passed his broker's exam and was now a licensed broker in New York State. I enjoyed seeing him booked and busy but also missed him as the summer months rolled in. My job was going well, and I couldn't complain. I had a few bumps in the road whilst living alone but could say overall, I was doing well.

One of the bumps in the road was going back and forth to court to settle with Julien. He'd proven to be relentless in his mission to not sell the house. I knew he was mostly doing it to spite me, but I wasn't sure what sense it made, him knowing he was overall happier with another woman.

I had yet to confront him about the very woman he was cheating on me with becoming his fiancée not long after he kicked me out of my house. I honestly didn't care at the point I'd reached. I was besotted with Johnathan, and it was the kind of love that made me forget Julien was even a part of my life. I was saddened in the grand scheme with how we ended but those were consequences of my actions that I knew in any timeline I wouldn't change. Julien always negates the fact that he was no angel either.

With all that aside, I had to admit that I was flourishing, and I wasn't mad at the growth. Also, my female friendships were something I both enjoyed and appreciated. I was growing closer with Lashawn and getting to know her on a personal level that I hadn't been privy to before. Not that I never wanted to, it just never happened. I just knew her enough that I loved her for Uriel.

I was currently at her house for a few drinks while Uriel was out working. We were chatting and watching bad reality television when she randomly said,

"I'm ready to get married and this nigga playing."

I raised a brow, thrown somewhat by the thought process. I shouldn't have been as we were watching reruns of Platinum Weddings on WeTV.

"How is he playing, Shawn?" I questioned, taking a sip. "You told him you're ready or you just waiting for him to catch a hint?"

"Hm. I'm unsure. I just feel like he should've looked at me and said self, we not losing this good pussy. But apparently, it's not good enough."

I've heard Uriel make up horrible songs about the aforementioned while he was drunk some time ago. So, I know that much to not be true. I mentioned that to her and made Lashawn weak with laughter.

"Don't say nothing because I wasn't supposed to say nothing," I cackled. "But I had to let you know that's not it."

Lashawn giggled. "Thanks for holding me down. I know you're basically the opp to the men nowadays but still."

I smiled sadly as that much was true. I used to be the cool girl that hung out with the lit guys but my becoming Johnathan's woman meant certain boundaries had been put up, even if not intentionally. I wasn't one of the guys any longer. Certain talk couldn't happen around me anymore, especially when Johnathan was present. We didn't even have certain conversations any longer now that we were together. Most of the time it'd spark jealousy.

"Yeah. I would've had to tell you regardless though."

"I appreciate you. Tell your boy I'm ready to get married though."

I laughed, taking another sip of my wine. I knew I didn't have a dog in that fight but wondered what was taking Uriel so long to propose. They'd been together for a few years and there was no real reason why he shouldn't. Lashawn was pretty much a man's dream from what I've been told, even by a jealous Julien a time or two. I used to reply back that Uriel also doesn't have a line of women claiming him to be theirs, either.

"You're not the one to have this talk with, anyway. I know you're not even in marriage mode at this point in time."

"No, not really. I'm not totally closed off to it, either... I'm whipped."

Lashawn barked out laughter. "I know you are. I've never seen you this...excited."

I smirked. "Excited?"

"You used to look, so sad, even when you were smiling. I...didn't ask questions, especially in the beginning of my relationship with L because I barely knew you. I knew it was one of those, mind ya business Shawn, moments but I could tell. The few times you bought that man around he was a pain and niggas just dealt with it because he was your man. I always loved you but...I wanted better for you. I'm glad you finally had enough and gave John a shot. The difference is night and day."

I smiled, knowing exactly what she was talking about. I felt the difference, too, but I didn't totally want to put it all on Johnathan. Ironically, Xander had something to do with it, too.

"Xander told me something before we left for the party that hit me hard. I think it's because out of everybody, Xan just stays out of the way..."

Lashawn nodded. That much was true about Xander. He handled his scandals and stayed out of the way and expected the same treatment from everybody else. I knew Julien had to be doing me bad if Xander had something to say about it.

"He told me I had to look at who I was and figure out if I wanted to keep taking Julien's bullshit. I had to realize I didn't have to keep doing it. And then...Johnathan showed me love in motion. In all the years I've known Julien...I can only count on one hand how many times he did something for my birthday. Johnathan and the boys always celebrate me. I think the only reason Julien found out I wasn't home that night was because the party pictures showed up on IG and mutual friends were posting like crazy. He knew it was up when I didn't answer my phone."

Lashawn cackled. "Good for his ass. It was just time, Key. I'm happy to see you happy. Now that you're happy though, it's time for me TO GET MARRIEDT!"

My laughter exploded at Lashawn's dramatics, but I also wondered if she was lowkey triggered because of Micah and Shaunte's breakup. It was still news that rocked us all being that the pair were together a long time. It'd been years since we all graduated from Clark so there was actually no reason why a proposal hadn't happened yet. Even Uriel had been ready to propose to Chantel when they'd been together during their happiest times.

I almost spat at the thought of her name but refrained from making a face. I didn't want to alarm Lashawn.

"I'm sure Uriel has plans for that, Shawn," I said. "I feel like other than Johnny, L is one of the last good ones. They honestly don't make them like him anymore. Y'all will be fine. Probably will propose before this year is out."

Now I was reaching but still, even if our relationship changed, I had to hold my boy down. Uriel was truly one of the few good men I knew in my life and I wouldn't change him for the world. Xander liked to call him bitch-made but Uriel was just an overall solid man. No trauma to get over. His parents were steady people who poured love into him and so he wanted to pour the same love into a loving partner.

My phone rang, the picture showing my man with all his beautiful features-dark brown eyes, chiseled face and strong jawline, not to mention those beautiful full lips-

staring back at me. I felt myself flush from inside out as I picked up the phone with almost no hesitation. Lashawn's cackle was soft this time and I playfully rolled my eyes.

"Johnny," I said. "What's up, baby?"

"I'm leaving the office. You got PTO time?"

"Why?"

"We're taking a quick trip to Long Island for the weekend. I have a house to show and prayerfully a deal to close all in one fell swoop. I think I should have my lady with me."

"Hm. Sounds like you just want some loving on demand."

He chuckled. "And if I did? I can't get that, baby?"

His voice dropped a couple decibels and I felt a tremor run down my spine. I bit my lip, forgetting Lashawn was there altogether.

"You know you can."

My voice was almost like a purr. It was almost a shame that he hadn't been in front of me because this would've been a moment to jump into his arms and...

"You know I need that..." he cleared his throat. "But there's going to be a showing and I have to host a party for prospective clients to be able to see the house. So, I'd love for you to be my date."

"I would love to."

"Good," he said. "Now about that..."

"About what?"

"That," he said. "Where you at?"

"Lashawn's."

"I'm sending an Uber for you," he said. "Shipping your sexy ass to my place. You good with that?"

"Mm-hmm."

"I'll see you there, baby."

Johnathan shared the ride information with me and noted that the cab would arrive in less than five minutes. I bit my lip once more and jumped when Lashawn called my name.

"Mm-hm. Talking nasty and shit in my house! Forgot I was there and everything!"

I laughed helplessly, popping Lashawn on the leg. I stood up, gathering my things and announced that I was getting ready to head out. She cackled and I shrugged my shoulders.

"Don't sit there judging me. You would do the same if it were you."

"And did, sis," Lashawn shrugged. "It's just so fun and refreshing to see you in this mood. A whole night and day difference."

"I know and I love it!" I squealed. "I need to start packing for this random ass trip he's taking me on."

"That's what y'all calling it? Preparing? Well, prepare your best and don't get caught up on being too perfect. Sometimes men like it a little messy."

Lashawn winked and I fell out laughing again. I blew air kisses at my friend and then stormed out of her apartment, her giggles following me out.

Friendship was a relationship most often underrated but somehow, I was grateful for Lashawn's.

Johnathan Barnes

"And who the fuck is James?"

I felt my face get hot while listening to my woman recount her story about asking her manager for time off. I saw the shock enter her eyes as she looked up from the water she was drinking into my eyes, probably at the sharpness of my tone.

The last few words she said to me had been that, *he granted me the time off but said I was going to have to make it up to him for being absent.* I knew the tone because I was a man and knew my woman was beautiful. Kiara didn't catch it because naïveté was her middle name in some moments. I still felt as if she should've known that the man was flirting with her but knew my love was missing the pieces of the puzzle. She wouldn't have confessed that much to me otherwise.

Kiara didn't know I'd find that man and beat the brakes off him. Damn the fact that her position was remote and it'd take me a few days to find him. I would.

"My boss?" She gasped, "He didn't mean anything by that, Johnny. He's playful."

"No, he's flirting and wondering why you haven't taken the bait after all the time you've been working there. He's trying to play work husband."

"No, he's not." She took another sip. "He's playful all around."

"So, he says shit like that to all the other women you work with?"

I'd been leaning on the counter and Kiara on the island. I was trying to give her a few seconds to enjoy the water before I wore her out but now I was feeling territorial, and she was playing obtuse so now I had to make her understand something.

Kiara was contemplative and quiet, probably trying to find an answer to my question that didn't exist. It made me smirk as I advanced on her, lifting her by the legs and sitting her in front of me on the counter. I eyed her, watching her swallow as I lifted her chin to look into my eyes fully.

"He doesn't. You know why? Because you're not all the other women. That nigga been plotting for the longest and you ain't been giving him airtime. Mostly because you ain't even know it was like that."

"I mean...say you're right. Why does that matter?"

"Because he has no business saying fly shit like that in the first place. If you'd been uncomfortable with it, that's an HR case. That and I might find the nigga and learn him somethin'."

My hand grabbed the back of her neck and stroked the side of it. I watched her bite her lip, my ministrations turning her on. The knowledge of that made me harden.

"I like my job, baby. So far, he hasn't posed a true problem and I hadn't seen it as flirting more than him joking around. Most bosses hate for their people to bang out on them."

I chuckled. "I hear you, baby. I just want you to hear me. That nigga better watch his step because I'll let him know. That's all I'm saying."

"Why? I can't have a work husband, Johnny?" she purred, reaching up to stroke my neck, "Competition make you antsy?"

I reached up and ran my fingers through her hair, gripping lightly at her roots. I smirked at her lowered lids and leaned in to kiss her full lips, groaning as I slid my tongue into her mouth.

"Stop fuckin' playing with me, Key." I pulled back, gripping the sides of her shirt, pulling it up and over her face. "Don't act like I won't hurt somebody over you..."

My kisses rained down her neck and over her chest. I pulled her bra straps down, not bothering to undo her bra. I let her breasts free and licked over her nipples one after the other. I alternated with my hands, enjoying her soft moans and keens.

I pulled back, undoing her jeans and helping her slide out of them. Tossing them on the floor, I pulled her panties to the side and pushed her backwards. I edged her legs open and leaned in, taking my fill of her. I stroked her middle with my tongue and reveled in her cries for more. I complied, pleased when I felt her release into my mouth. Her shudders made me groan as my name reached my ears. I reached up, grabbing her breasts and stroking her nipples, thinking of the erotic picture she made on my kitchen island, almost but not quite naked yet still a total mess for me.

"Your work husband do it for you like me?"

I growled, licking her all over again, building her back up to the climax I hadn't even let her release from in the first place. Her gasps were my answer, but I wasn't satisfied. I pulled back just when her cries started to pitch more.

"What work husband?"

Her eyes were lowered and she was biting her lip. I felt myself harden even more at the sight of her, looking like pure sex from my vantage point. I was weak in front of her but for the moment she would think I was in the dominant position. Still, I wasn't about to let another man see my woman like this. I gritted my teeth at the thought that another man was even imagining my woman like this.

"James. That nigga you said was my competition?"

I hadn't let her answer. I went back to work, working her over until curse words were escaping her. I chuckled as I pulled away, delaying her orgasm once more.

"Baby, please."

"Please what?" I asked, standing up, towering over her. "Let that pussy come? Tell your work husband to do it."

Kiara reached back and undid her bra. She slipped her panties off and tossed them on the floor. Sliding back, she opened her legs farther for me, reaching in between them and started to play with herself. One hand in between her legs and one holding her breast. She flicked at her nipple and I watched as she threw her head back with a moan. I watched, suddenly aching with need.

"I don't have to get anyone to do it because I can do it for myself. But the one man who turns me on in the world is you..."

She moaned as the feeling got good to her all over again. Dipping a finger into herself, she swirled it around and then pulled it out, easing it into my mouth. I sucked her juices off her finger and groaned.

"Stop being jealous, baby. I want for you. I ache for you. There's nobody else but you. Now make me come, Johnny."

Suddenly, I forgot I was playing jealousy games.

I cursed, dropping my pants and my boxers. In one fell swoop, I snatched my woman to the edge of the counter and eased my way inside of her. Her moan caused me to curse and hold her steady before I pulled out and eased in again. My hand buried itself into her hair again while I worked her over. My name, a litany on her lips, urged me on to bring her to paradise. Her shudder and cries were my reward and suddenly, I wanted more.

"Forgive me, baby. Sometimes I get jealous."

Kiara hadn't answered me. She only wrapped her legs around me as I picked her up off the counter and made my way to my bedroom. Her kisses along my neck made me feel as if she hadn't even heard me until she leaned up to lick my earlobe. I shuddered as I walked up the stairway and groaned as she did it again.

"You don't have to be jealous. It's only you, baby. Always has been. Always will be."

It was on that note that we kissed in front of my bedroom door. It was a passionate wrestle of our tongues. I was sure that our lips were swollen when we pulled away from each other.

"Now make love to me, baby. I need it."

"Say no more."

I crossed the room, laid her on the bed and entered her once more. We hadn't stopped until neither one of us could go another inch.

Chapter Nine

Kiara David

"So, I met a man."

Shaunte made the announcement while I served her, Lashawn, and Tasha wine at my place. I was giddy with excitement as I'd already had one cup before they arrived, but the bomb Shaunte dropped on us was unexpected. Almost as unexpected as LaTasha's presence in our lives again.

LaTasha Morgan looked different from when I met her in high school. We didn't run in the same circles but the crush she'd had on Xander wasn't a secret. Xander never made a move being that she wasn't his taste back then, but one fateful night brought them together and I was still reeling from watching my friend.

He was in love and couldn't be saved.

I never felt protective over any of my friends but seeing Xander's heart for Tasha definitely made mine a little tender to him. He tried for a relationship years ago and before he could propose one to the girl, he found out he was a part of a rotation. Then Xander suddenly had a new rotation. It was a sad day however because that girl reinforced his beliefs that women weren't worth the trouble.

It was easy to see how Xander had gotten caught up though. Tasha was beautiful. Her skin was dark and smooth. No imperfection could be seen on her skin. Her eyes were almond shaped and dark. Her waist was small but everything else on her was thick. The only other thing small was her nose.

She was a nurse which was phenomenal. I wasn't sure how she stayed beautiful and did her job, but I was a fan. Tasha was very classy and reserved until someone upset her. Then she was ready for war. I liked that about her, mostly because she fit in well with us. It was cool to reunite with someone in a new way and wondered where our friendship would take us.

"You met a man? Oh, shit," Lashawn giggled, taking a sip. "How do we feel about this man?"

Shaunte smirked. "Like I like him, a lot."

"So, who's the mystery man? I noticed you'd been hiding for a little while," I said, taking my own sip.

"Bitch, you noticed between getting dick coming out your ears with John?" Lashawn teased. "Don't sit here and lie."

"I ain't gotta lie," I shrugged. "Besides, how are you talking about me when I know what you be doing to my boy?"

"We're not talking about me," Lashawn shrugged. "We're talking about Tay right now."

Shaunte cackled. "Y'all stop."

"I'm just saying, sis," Lashawn shrugged. "All jokes aside, who is this man? You've been mum on giving a name, address, blood type."

Shaunte smirked. “You trying to steal my man, Shawn? L not up to par these days?”

Lashawn rolled her eyes. “Again, we’re talking about you, sis.”

Shaunte raised a quiet brow at the rebuff, but we knew what that meant. For whatever reason, Uriel was in the doghouse and until Lashawn felt better about whatever he was doing, he was going to live there. I was tempted to change the subject but knew the moment wasn’t right. Besides, I was still curious about Shaunte’s random revelation.

“Anyway,” Shaunte started. “I’ve known him for a while actually. He used to try to get at me at my old job before I quit. Then I bumped into him at the Apple store and he bought my air pod pros.”

“Oh?” I rose a brow. “That’s a flex. So, he’s throwing money at it?”

“A lot of money,” Shaunte answered, playing in her hair. “And a lot of dick. I’ve done a lot of crying over the past few months.”

“Months?”

Lashawn had taken the words out of my mouth before I could say anything. I was as flabbergasted as anyone else in the room, except for Tasha. Tasha listened intently, but I could tell she was enjoying the tale by the look on her face and the slow way she sipped her wine.

“Months, sis, I hear that. Come on, tell us more,” Tasha prompted. “Is he giving you that soul wrenching dick?”

"Wrenching, okay?!" Shaunte squealed. "I...I've never had nothing like that in my life. And it honestly doesn't matter what I'm feeling like, he'll drop the money for us to go. And most of the time, I'm just throwing an arrow on a map and seeing whether he's down or not."

"So...what happens to Mike?" I questioned. "I thought you were holding out for him?"

Shaunte shrugged. "I don't mean disrespect, Key, but... what about him?"

Lashawn mumbled a low curse word and I wrung my hands a little bit. I could tell she was over him by the look in her eyes. I couldn't really argue for my friend but also, I had to try. Still, there was no argument I could bring up in his defense. He'd given the crew nothing to base an argument off of.

From the little Johnathan told me, Micah had a full rotation of women. From Xander's proud declaration there was a different woman every night. He was out living his best life and there were no signs of him slowing down. One month there was one set of women. Another month, there was a new set of women. I wasn't sure whether Xander's influence was to blame or not, but I'd be hard pressed to say that there wasn't any effect at all.

When Shaunte's name came up amid his friends, he'd shrug her off and keep right on trucking. I knew the advice given to him had fallen on deaf ears. Was he affected by their breakup? Certainly. However, I was pretty sure my friend was going to keep indulging until the doors closed on him to make things happen with Shaunte.

"I know you're trying to defend your friend but Key... fuck that. Micah and I were basically married for many years. I damn near played his second mama. I think the most grown thing that man has done in all our years was ask me out in the eighth grade. Everything after? I was raising a man. Now he's smelling himself and if I hadn't taken care of myself for the most part in my years with him? What would I have to show for it? As it were, there's no ring."

Lashawn was stunned into silence. I had no more defense because she was absolutely right. Micah hadn't cheated on her but as far as making the moves he was supposed to, none were made, and we were all past thirty. I knew the only reason Johnathan hadn't gotten on bended knee yet was because of me wanting to deal with my issues. Also, I wanted to enjoy a good man before I had a good husband.

At this point Micah was just having his cake and eating it, too.

"It's giving, I got to put myself first, Lucious," Tasha said. "I ain't mad at you. No use spending your good years on a nigga who's not about that action. That's what you need."

"I'm glad somebody feels it. These two acting like they don't know what's going on."

"Don't do that," I laughed. "It's like you said, Mike is my friend. He was your friend and shit too at first."

"He's been my man longer," Shaunte said. "What's your excuse, Shawn?"

"I just knew you been with the nigga forever so to see you talking your shit is wild right now. Am I mad at you, though? No. Uriel might be sitting right next to his ass he keeps fuckin' around."

Now my eyes bugged out and I almost asked Lashawn what was wrong but she waved me off, catching the concern on my face. I was also concerned because Shaunte's bitterness was translating into fear in Lashawn. There was no denying after the comment she made and then remembering our other conversation.

"Don't do Uriel," I said, ignoring her. "Shaunte is Shaunte, and you are you, Shawn."

"We still talking about-"

"Nah sis, that ship sailed. We know it's clipped for Mike. Still might not be in the long run if he finds some sense."

I tossed one more look at Shaunte who shook her head in the negative.

"I'm just saying whatever's going on, don't have my boy out here looking bad. He's in love with you, Shawn. Whatever's going on, fix it."

"It's not on me to fix, Key. It's on him. I'm just giving y'all a warning unlike Ms. Aldana in the corner looking smug off her new rich man."

Shaunte shrugged. "I mean it's not only about his money. It's...more. It's the sense of him knowing what he wants from me and not playing games. I know in the long run I can expect marriage and children and an actual home in the next few years. Micah doesn't have direction, but he has wandering eyes and the nerve to ask me when I stopped being fun. That's pretty much where it's at for me. The question you have to ask is if your man has vision or if you're a placeholder?"

It was then that I heard my bell ring. I furrowed my face, walking over to my intercom. I wasn't expecting anyone but knew inwardly if it was my man, I was kicking everybody out. Or, at the very least I hoped that they all caught the hint and went about their day. I was on the fast track to tipsiness anyway.

I pressed the button and asked who it was. Surely enough, my man's voice bounced back to me. Though excited, I was confused and mumbled that much as I buzzed him in. The snickers hit my ears, but I dutifully ignored them.

"Whatever you want...it's alright with me...'cause you got that whip appeal..." Lashawn started singing.

The rest of them joined in and I actively ignored them as I waited for the knock on the door. I could care less because I've seen all my friends in love. I looked at Tasha even now and knew that even after all the time that's gone, Xander was still the center of her universe. It was just cool to make fun of me now.

I heard two knocks on the door and in walked Johnathan and to my surprise, Uriel. Lashawn's eyes widened and her face flushed, and it caused me to get upset realizing that Johnathan helped his friend ambush mine in what should have been a safe place. I looked over at Lashawn and hoped she read the confusion in my face because I didn't even know they were in a heavy disagreement until about two hours ago.

"Hey y'all. What's up?"

Johnathan greeted everybody and I eyed him. He looked repentant and I knew he was only trying to help his friend. He hadn't known that he was crashing girl's time. Uriel hadn't known either, but I knew my friend. Whatever mission he was on, he was ten toes down and there was no turning back. It caused me to sigh inwardly.

"Lashawn," He said. "Come on, baby, let's go."

"Go where? I'm going back to mama's after this so you might as well go ahead and go home."

"I'm not going without you."

His voice was authoritative. I saw the shiver run down my friend's back and knew she was fighting a losing battle. I saw the moment her eyes grew soft. All that hot stuff she was talking about earlier was now a moot point and it was actually my turn to sing whip appeal. Still, I'd have mercy on my girl. Whatever issues she had with Uriel could be worked on. I didn't want to have Shaunte and Micah Part Two if they could salvage their love.

"Baby, I'm not going without you. We need to talk this shit out. I want my woman back home."

Lashawn bit her lip, then nodded, and then got up and gave each of us a chaste kiss on the cheek. She grabbed her things and walked over to Uriel, allowing him to take her hand and lead her out of the door. I sighed heavily as my other two friends grabbed their things and called it a night. I rolled my eyes as the door shut and turned my ire onto Johnathan.

"Johnathan...what the fuck?!"

"I'm sorry, baby. I didn't know that it was everybody. I just thought it was y'all two. L called me and asked if you'd heard from her, and I was like yeah...pretty sure they're chilling today. So, he's telling me he needs to see her and I'm like aight, bet. They just going through a rough patch, so I figured he was ready to apologize because we all know he was wrong."

I sighed, running a hand down my face. I looked up into my boyfriend's handsome face and shook my head at his thought process.

"I wish you'd have texted me first."

"Nah. Either way it wouldn't work and you know that. L wants his woman back home so he's going to get her back home."

"I still wished you would've texted, Johnathan," I said, rolling my eyes.

"Hm, what happened to Johnny?"

Johnathan mimicked the soft way my voice trills when I shorten his name in only the way I do it. I giggled, flipping him off so he knew he was wrong for just pulling up with his friend in tow.

I started cleaning up my space, picking up my wine glasses and settling them in the sink. Johnathan helped me grab the wine bottles. He put them in my recyclable bin and then turned to me as I rolled my eyes at him again and went about washing my glassware.

I stilled when I felt his arms encircle my waist but kept washing. He chuckled lightly and leaned in, laying kisses on my neck.

"So, you're going to be mad at me? I thought L was your boy?"

"He is, but we were having girl time. If y'all had waited, we could've softened her up just a little bit more. I could tell she was thinking about talking to him but no, y'all Neanderthals just going to come in and ambush the situation. I should've known better because you always call before you come through. Why I thought you were just surprising me, I have no clue."

Johnathan waited until I put the last glass face down on my drying mat before he turned me around and lifted my face. I inwardly cursed, knowing I forgave him by the contriteness I read in his eyes.

"You right, baby. I'm sorry. I admit that I also did it out of selfishness. They've been beefing for about two weeks, and I was the one who had to hear about it. It...it was starting to get bad. I would've done anything to get him right...being that all I had to do was give up Lashawn's location? I was doing it. I'm sorry I didn't alert you though. I got you next time."

I giggled, shaking my head at the apology.

"I'm also upset because I don't want her to think I was in on that. I don't like ambushing people."

Johnathan chuckled, tilting my face up to look into his. He stroked my chin.

"You don't have to worry about that. That deer-caught-in-headlights expression you had was enough evidence that you were innocent."

I smirked and attempted to pull out of his arms when I found he had me bound to him.

"Let me go, Johnny," I giggled, "You on time out."

"Well, I'm Johnny again, so that's a start. How do I get out of time out?"

Johnathan leaned in, kissing along my jawline, up to my ear. I moaned when he pulled my lobe into his mouth, nipping it before pulling back and looking into my eyes. I felt myself flush, taking in the earnest look on his face. I bit my lip, shaking my head in the negative, doing my best not to give in but at that point, I wasn't even sure what I was fighting at this point.

"I can't get out, baby?"

He continued his ministrations on the other side, kissing my cheeks lightly until he reached my mouth. He kissed my lips lightly until I began kissing him back and allowed his tongue to massage mine slowly and methodically. I became putty in his hands while he apologized for the slight without words.

His arms loosened and I enclosed my arms around his neck and pulled him in closer. I wondered within myself what was it about him that made me forgive him so easily? I pulled away, looking into his eyes.

Johnathan surprised me by picking me up by my waist. I wrapped my legs around his waist and tightened my hold around his neck. I enjoyed the strength I felt in his arms and surprised myself by leaning in and kissing him back. Pulling away, I sighed, laying a hand on his cheek.

"How do you do that?"

"Do what?"

His voice was thick with lust. I ignored the hum in between my legs, already spurred on by the wine mixed by my own need for him.

"I meant to stay mad at you. Now I almost can't remember why I was upset."

"Hm. I'm not too prideful to beg for your forgiveness," he said. "Whatever I have to do to get it, I'm going to do it. I don't like my baby mad at me."

To drive his point home, he slid me his tongue once more and we kissed, slowly. I felt the shivers run down my back and pulled away.

"So, how do I make it up to you?"

It was a phrase I wasn't used to hearing so I didn't even know what to say. To be fair however, I just didn't want my friend upset at me over the shenanigans. As much as I wanted her and Uriel to work out, I didn't want her to feel pressured into doing it either. Lashawn was someone I felt would always be in my life whether she and Uriel worked out or not. Her as a person was just so top tier and I didn't want her to feel as if her trust was betrayed.

Still, I understood where Johnathan was coming from with Uriel, too. So that much allowed me to let go of my anger-tinged fears. I wouldn't have my man crawling on his knees for my forgiveness over something trivial. It was probably high time they talked anyway.

"There's nothing to make up for," I answered. "You hungry?"

"I'm good, baby. I'm looking for something to drink."

"What you want? I got water, some apple juice, and some w-"

"-you, baby. I want to drink you."

I felt my face flush and my heartbeat double as the words left his mouth sexily. I leaned in, rewarding him with a kiss. His thick lips pressed back, and his fingers curled through my hair.

"Let me get a sip."

I giggled as he walked me toward my room and laid me on my bed. I wasn't sure how my bottoms disappeared as quickly as they had but Johnathan got comfortable and drank. He drank until he was good and full. I saw stars. I might've even seen the moon. It was enough to make my eyes blurry each time an orgasm swept through me. Every swipe of his tongue told me he was willing to risk it all just to get to this moment.

There was a moment when our eyes locked as he looked at me and I looked at him. His love for me was deep and though I had a working idea, I truly had no clue.

Johnathan Barnes adored me.

He never had to whisper those same words as he kissed all over my body. My clothes disappeared, inch by inch but his lips covered me in a reverence I never experienced before. Not that my boyfriend list was long, but it was crazy how what one man failed to give me, one delivered effortlessly.

It was what made me push him back on my bed and slide down his member and love on him slowly. I looked into his eyes as I confessed without words that I loved him. That I appreciated him. That he hadn't been the only one longing for the other. It seemed to be the recurring theme, but I found new reasons all the time to love him.

I came down from my high and giggled as Johnathan pulled me close to him, taking another kiss from my lips.

"That wasn't a sip, greedy," I giggled, kissing his lips once more. "That was a gulp."

"You taste good."

He chuckled at his corny response before nuzzling my nose with his nose. I flushed as he looked into my eyes, deeply.

"I love how you open up for me," he said. "I always thought you'd be a dream to be with, but you've blown away my expectations. You're so lovely, baby."

"It's only for you, Johnny," I whispered. "I might've been with someone else but...it wasn't the same as this. Not by a long shot. It's like I've never been with anybody but you."

The impish grin he wore at my confession made me slap him lightly on the chest. His chuckles washed over me before his kiss laid on my forehead.

"Forgive me, baby. That was a strong compliment. I had to have my moment."

"Mhm," I said. "Whatever."

Johnathan kissed me again.

"I love you, Kiara David."

"I love you, Johnathan Barnes."

"Always?"

"Put a pinkie promise on it."

Our pinkies were linked until we fell asleep as the sun cast its golden glow in my room.

Johnathan Barnes

That'd probably been the last lovely moment I shared with my love for weeks on end. One thing came after the other and it made me wonder why the honeymoon period couldn't last longer.

I honestly had Micah to thank for setting things in motion. I wasn't even sure how he ended up at my place, but he'd been the one to push the first domino and make everything tumble down.

It'd been a perfect evening. I got my woman to spend the night with me after a long week and I'd been rearing up to deep dive into her love. She was looking beautiful as usual as she cooked us a pot roast. I'd been salivating for it as the smell filled up the house.

We shared our meal and a few glasses of wine. Kiara was delightfully tipsy, and I was enjoying her affection. She'd been straddling me, happily feeding me her tongue and I'd been getting drunk off her love. I'd been getting ready to palm her breast in my hand when the bell rang.

The action caused me to pause and look into her eyes in confusion. She looked back at me, just as confused. I tapped her leg lightly and she stood up, covering herself up in the process. Whatever lacy number she'd donned for me, I wasn't going to see it that night. All hopes that I'd be able to were dashed in the sand when I reached my door.

Micah was singing Loyal at the top of his lungs at my doorway. The song became apparent the more his off key singing reached my ears. It caused me to groan, a curse word leaving my lips as I snatched open the door.

"Mike, what the fuck, man?"

My friend stumbled in, still singing the tune at the top of his lungs and I knew my night had just gone into the toilet.

"What the fuck what? I'm just here to share the gospel truth that these hoes ain't loyal, nigga. Get out while you can."

Micah chuckled, stumbling into the living room. He caught Kiara's eye as she finished buttoning her shirt and halfway smirked at her.

"What up, Key? You still giving my nigga the run-a-round?" he chuckled. "Your homegirl teaching you how to drain him for everything he got before you leave, too?"

Kiara rose a brow. "Micah, chill out. I'm not the one you're mad at."

"I should be. Y'all chicks play too many games, man. Make a nigga chase it. Make a nigga wait for it and then you drain the nigga of every bit of life before you decide you good."

"Stop talking about my friend like that, Mike. Whatever's going on, you fucked that up!" Kiara snapped. "Not me. Not her. You."

"Fuck you, Key. Like you're so smart. Letting this punk ass nigga dog you out for years, now suddenly, you want Johnathan to be your man? You knew this nigga wanted you and you stayed with the other nigga."

Micah chuckled and the sound made my skin crawl. I knew how he was making the situation sound, even as Kiara turned to me, hurt pouring out of her eyes. There were no tears but there didn't even need to be any. I walked over to Kiara, reaching out for her hand. When I'd been close to picking it up, she snatched her hand away, shaking her head at me.

"Don't do that to me, baby," I said. "Listen, I'm going to call an uber for you, I got to take care of Micah."

"So, you're going to put me out in favor of this nigga?" she motioned to him. "No, fuck him and fuck you, Johnathan! I'll get my own uber."

I rolled my eyes, calling the cab. I knew I had to separate them because the situation was volatile. Micah decided to pick on my woman while he was drunk and Kiara couldn't separate logic from her own emotions. It was a recipe for disaster, and I didn't want things to escalate. If Micah moved the wrong way I was going to have to step in and I didn't want our friendship to crumble on account of a fight.

Still, I wasn't sure that the words he said to Kiara didn't bother me. I knew what was troubling my love. A drunk tongue speaking sober thoughts. It was looking shaky for their friendship, mostly because Micah probably thought of her that way in reality.

When the Uber showed up, I walked Kiara to the door. When she looked up at me, her eyes were glittery with tears.

"Baby, stop. I have to take care of this. I'll call you."

"Hm. Maybe you shouldn't."

I rose a brow, shutting the door slightly and blocking her path from getting inside. She looked at me pointedly.

"Baby...you know he's drunk. He's barely going to remember he said any of that in the morning."

"But he said it and you did nothing about it. That's what's hurting me, Johnathan."

Her voice cracked on my name and I sighed, opening the door. I had to accept that part as my failure, but I was trying to rectify the slight as much as I could. It took everything in me not to pull her out of the car.

"Text me when you get home."

Kiara eyed me like she wanted to fight some more but settled in the seat. I slammed her door and watched the cab retreat to her destination.

I sighed, walking back in the house to see Micah grinning as if he won the lottery. I rose a brow, wondering what he found so funny. I questioned him, suddenly in a mood.

"You found some sense and let that go? You were looking crazy these past few months."

"Crazy?"

"Nigga, spending your bread like water. Being in love with this chick for years and she acting like she didn't know it. Man, please. If you ain't her number one choice, why would you pursue that?"

I crossed my arms, almost falling for the bait. I knew to a degree Micah felt that way but also, I knew that something between him and Shaunte was broken. I sighed, running a hand down my face, exhaustion suddenly filling every part of my body. I pulled my phone out and shot a text to Uriel and Xander. I didn't want to go down this road alone.

Uriel had hit me back up saying get somebody else to do it. I sucked my teeth softly, looking up into the pitiful eyes of one of my best friends.

"Let's talk about you and Shaun, because this is what this is about. Not me and Kiara," I said. "What's wrong with you, nigga? You fouled out?"

Micah sucked his teeth. "Her stupid ass left. For what I don't even know. We were good! I don't even understand the noises she was making about me not being with her."

"You don't?" I questioned, calmly. "Any man that loves a woman he's with follows behind her when she gives chase. There's no way Kiara could ever say she wants to leave and I'm not on her ass, respectfully."

"So, I'm supposed to just crawl back after she leaves?"

Xander texted me that he was on the way, and I almost shed a grateful tear. I wasn't sure how much more of Micah's drunk thoughts I could take.

Also, it made perfect sense that it should be Xander to come to the rescue. Micah played the part for a few months faking like he was a playboy and now his woman was in the arms of another man. That had to be the reason overall for this man to be belligerent and acting the fool in my place of residence.

Micah started singing Loyal again and I walked away, leaving him to his own diversions. I ended up in the kitchen, pouring him a cup of water before returning and shoving the glass in his hand.

"Drink, bitch ass nigga," I mumbled, partially forcing the water down his throat. "And shut your ass up."

Micah wiped his mouth with a dopey smile. Some of the water made it on his shirt. He wiped off the excess from his lips and continued singing.

Micah started laughing to himself and mumbling. He attempted standing up, but his body was too heavy and that much caused me to sigh. I needed him in his own house and not in mine. I hoped Xander showed up before long.

My doorbell rang about thirty minutes later. I opened my door and was grateful to see both of my friends. Xander looked guilty and Uriel looked annoyed. It reminded me that we were a true brotherhood, and nobody got left behind in our circle. No matter how stupid they were.

Xander offered up his truck and they hauled Micah to the backseat. I rode next to Micah while Uriel and Xander rode in the front. I sighed as the singing died down. I'd grown tired of it quickly.

"What's wrong, nigga? She got engaged on your ass?"

Uriel was the one who questioned him this time. Micah sighed deeply, and I was sorry that Uriel was right. I knew the question was in jest, but he'd hit the nail on the head. That made sense for why he was acting the way he was. Still, I started to feel an ache in my heart as I replayed some of what he said to me. I wondered if my friend really felt that way or if his words were just hurt filled thoughts because the window of opportunity to get Shaunte back closed on him.

"Yeah, nigga. Got engaged on me like I wasn't good to her for my whole life. My whole life!"

Uriel sighed and I heard his reproof in that single expulsion of air. It was how I felt. I was waiting for Xander to say something, but he drove on quietly, his face scrunched up in contemplative thought. I was waiting for him to at least apologize for the part he had to play in the situation. Still, I was torn. Surely, Micah still had to own up for the fact that he had gotten caught up following his own inclinations. I hated to say it but something in my friend caused Shaunte to slow them down.

She'd been testing him, and he failed. I didn't know Shaunte as well as anybody else, but I knew that she was inclined to test out a situation every now and again. In the past, Micah had been a worthy partner. Presently, he wasn't making the moves he should have as her man and their long history was no longer enough in her eyes to stay.

Kiara crossed my mind again and I sighed, running a hand down my face. Micah's words stung her badly and I was certain she felt as if I'd chosen a side. I was apologetic that I couldn't handle the situation the way she would have preferred, however, my friend was hurting and I knew it would escalate with his state of mind. I had to protect everybody involved, even at the cost of my own comfort. It was something I hoped she understood once I reached back out to her. It wouldn't have been the first time we had disagreements, but it'd always been easy for us to get back on track. I was always willing to get back into her good graces.

The same applied here but I knew my baby was hurt by me and Micah. I had to figure out a way to make it right but make her understand how I had to move.

Xander pulled up to Micah's house and everyone but me helped him inside. I had to finally admit that I was disappointed in how he carried on earlier. I was insulted at how he came for my girl. Doubly disappointed because they were friends. I suddenly understood on a deeper level what Kiara meant when she felt I took his side and cursed lowly.

It was sometimes hard for me to realize that the dynamic changed entirely once we'd gotten together. Though for the most part she was still treated as the lady of our group, she was my lady first. There'd no longer be times when we all got together to shoot the shit. There were no longer times when we'd all gather together to watch a game. Getting together to play ball was a thing of the past because of our changed dynamic. To the boys, Kiara wasn't just the cool girl that we hung out with any longer. She was now my girl. They were all acting accordingly but me. Even down to Kiara, who knew to speak up for Shaunte in her friend's absence.

While Kiara loved Uriel like an older brother, she'd been concerned about my movements making Lashawn distrust her. The more she was leaning into her womanhood, Kiara was learning loyalty on another level as it pertained to her female relationships. I knew the betrayal came because she wouldn't have let any of them disrespect me without checking them for it. Now I was looking like the dudes who started podcasts because they were against everything women stood for and I was embarrassed.

The twosome stepped out of Micah's house about twenty minutes later. Uriel and Xander looked tired, and

I suddenly felt guilty for not helping them at all. I was getting ready to apologize when Xander chuckled dryly.

"Nah...you good, bro. I already know that nigga said some sideways shit before we got there so I understand why you stayed out here. I almost dumped this nigga on the floor after he started talking about he disappointed that I got with Tasha. But I'm chilling because I know some of this shit my fault."

Uriel chuckled. "Yeah. I'm glad you said it. We tried to make the nigga see reason and here you go, X."

"You right," Xander said. "But still, only a little bit. I can't make a nigga do what he ain't already wanted to do. I saw it in his eyes that he wanted to see what it was like. He enjoyed it more than I did. He knew it was time to settle down but wasn't ready. That's all this shit is about. It's just getting corny that he's blaming everybody but himself."

I shook my head, still embarrassed at my actions. I ran a hand down my face.

"My girl not fuckin' with me right now behind this nigga."

"Then make it right, John," Uriel said. "It's not rocket science. You just not used to shit being your fault but once you decide you're down for someone, then shit is your fault all the time now."

Uriel started laughing more fully at one of the jokes I would say all the time. However, it was only funny when I was saying it to him.

"So, you sent her home and called us to heave-ho this nigga?" Xander laughed. "I'm new to this relationship shit and know your ass was wrong. I can tell you one thing, Jay, there's no such thing as helping cry baby ass niggas when you getting right with yours. Again, I admit my bullshit in the scenario but he's a grown ass man that could've reflected over his choices and said, Xander I'm going to chill on this shit and make it up to mines."

Xander drove for a few more minutes quietly and then sighed. "Misery loves company, man. You think that nigga happy to see any of us happy? I finally found a woman I can take seriously. Uriel got him someone and you and Key finally made it happen. All this shit he's spewing is not meant to be taken seriously."

"Key hurt behind some of the shit he said," I groaned. "I should've punched him in the mouth, but I know on one level he's hurting."

"Why'd you open the door when his ass showed up anyway?" Uriel asked. "I'm not sending my woman home to be lonely and horny, Johnathan. Nigga you better see to your woman and make the shit right."

"She ain't fuckin' with me right now," I said. "I'm gonna give her some space."

"So you can be Micah Number Two?"

Xander's voice was incredulous, and the tone made me laugh against my will.

"Nah, nigga. It was hard enough carrying Micah's ass up to his room. I'm not carrying your big, drunk ass anywhere if Kiara decides to move on."

Still laughing, I said, "My man, I'm not giving her as much space as Micah gave Shaun. I'm going to see about mines. Just not tonight."

Uriel cursed. “Drop this nigga off to Kiara’s. I’ll grab an uber from there.”

“Take me home,” I said. “I’ll pull up the next morning and make it up.”

“Have it your way.”

Xander dropped me at the front of my house and then he and Uriel drove home in their separate vehicles. I toyed with the idea of pulling up to my love’s house and then called her. My calls kept going to voicemail. I sighed, the magnitude of what I’d done crashing down on me. I was even more embarrassed when Uriel explained his thoughts on it.

I texted her that I was pulling up in the morning and that I loved her before walking through the house. I turned off the pot roast and waited for it to cool before I put it away. It smelled divine and I was tempted to sneak a bite but something about not sharing the meal with the woman who cooked it didn’t sit well.

I dragged myself to bed, sighing as I looked over at the empty space next to me and cursed before laying down to rest. I was truly remorseful about what I allowed to happen and decided I would make it up to her as quickly as possible.

Chapter Ten

Kiara David

I walked into Starbucks the next morning, immediately spotting Julien in the corner next to a window. I rolled my eyes as he watched me walk towards him expectantly. I settled in the seat across from him as he wore a shit-eating grin.

"You don't look too happy to see me, Kiara. I thought we had good times together. I deserve at least a smile."

I rolled my eyes again. "Just say what you need to say. You only have five minutes to get your point across."

"Hm. You can play tough if you want but I know you miss a nigga. Mr. Barnes not all you thought he was, hm?"

"What makes you say that? There's nothing wrong with us."

Of course I was lying through my teeth because I was still hurt by my man, but it wasn't enough for me to pack up and leave. I had just wanted to calm down for a moment because the whole situation had gotten messy. I was more hurt by Micah than Johnathan's part. I knew that he just wanted to get his friend some help. I just didn't like that I was put out of the way because of it. I hated that Johnathan hadn't told Micah where to go with all the mess he was talking. Drunk or not, he had blatantly disrespected me like we hadn't been friends for many years. The slight wasn't an easy one to get over, but I wasn't announcing any breakup of the sort. I hadn't even jumped out the window that quickly over the subhuman that sat before me, so I wasn't going to do it over Johnathan.

Julien grinned and pulled up a story that Micah posted on Instagram. I was suddenly seeing red because of the message he put again reiterating that Johnathan would be making the right move by leaving me alone. My heart started to ache again because I did nothing for Micah to act out this way. I was confused on how I became a sudden target of his.

"Your boy is saying differently to me," Julien pressed. "I mean, don't even sweat it. I know I haven't always been the best man to you, Key. I can admit that. If you apologize for cheating on me with dude, I'll let you move back in. That's not even a problem."

I looked at Julien with a blank face and before I could stop myself, I started to laugh. The laugh came from the deepest part of my belly. I knew before I stopped laughing that my belly would ache for a short time due to the joke that my ex-boyfriend just told me. I shook my head, fanning my face as Julien's face took on a slight tinge of embarrassment from my reaction.

When I finally sobered up, I looked him in the eye, my own face hardening at his audacity.

"Julien. I'm glad you can admit to what we already knew. You were a monster. But, running around on me during college and embarrassing me on a daily basis? I should've left you then. Then, screwing your secretary for many years and then proposing to her right after you kicked me out of our home? That was bullshit. You act like you were upset that Johnny and I got together and that wasn't even the case. You just wanted to put on a show so you could move her on in. You had a legitimate reason to put me out. Before you had none, but you made this shit extra messy, Julien. All you needed to do was come to an agreement with me to sell and now we're in court."

I sighed, looking into his eyes and seeing the real reason for the visit. I wondered when this man was going to stop playing mind games on people? I wondered when he was going to stop going out of his way to lie and gaslight to get what he wanted. It was a mystery that I didn't even care to solve.

"Speaking of court, Julien, I'm not on the outs with Johnathan so much that I would beg your forgiveness. Even if we don't work out, I'm never going back to you. Fuck your forgiveness and fuck you. I want my fucking money, Julien. That's the best apology you could give me. My fucking money. I'll see you in court."

I stood up, anger flowing through my body. It was tempting to walk back over to Julien and spit in his face for what he was proposing to me.

I'd been settling to head back into an uber when a text message dinged. My heart pounded to see that it came from Johnathan. A small smile pulled on my face, swiping to see it until I actually read it. When I had, tears pooled in my eyes.

I know I wasn't right baby but to see you laughing it up with dude inside of Starbucks is crazy to me. I deserve better than that.

My heart started to ache because he'd gotten it so wrong. I wondered when he walked in and saw me and why he didn't just ask why I was there. Still, I could understand that the optics were bad.

I picked up my phone to call him and kept getting sent to voicemail. I left my message, deciding to give my man that much courtesy although at the point I was standing at, I didn't want to give any. He still had yet to even show up at my door to apologize for the ruckus the night before. The assumption that I would run back so easily to Julien's arms hurt me almost as bad as Micah's degradation of me.

Once my uber pulled up, I slid inside, wiping my tears that were fast falling. My man was over me and it seemed I actually had to go through a whole break up of both the love of my life and my best friend. Still, I'd go through the stages and move on. It was apparent that I wasn't going to win no matter what I did in the eyes of this circle.

Johnathan Barnes

Uriel was grinning ear to ear as he announced to us all that he'd finally proposed to Lashawn. I felt my own smile pull as his happiness was infectious. All three of us dapped him up and then settled in his living room. Xander started asking questions and I smirked, thinking it was crazy when the playboy of the group suddenly wanted to be an honest man himself. I was struggling in my heart as far as it came to Kiara and wasn't sure what to make of what I'd seen the other day.

I'd been walking inside of Starbucks to get her favorite drink and snacks and show up to her door to apologize. I'd been at the counter, getting ready to make the order when I heard her laughter.

I followed the sound to see her laughing loudly. I could tell it came from her belly and that was enough to incite jealousy. I already didn't want another man making her laugh like that but to see Julien on the other side of the table from her broke me down. I knew I had fouled up, but I don't think I fouled up that bad for her to be giving him airtime. I was grateful neither one of them saw me. I didn't want her to come to me with any lies about what I'd seen in the moment.

"Aye, why you over there looking despondent and shit?"

I looked up at Xander and started chuckling. The question came out of left field as Uriel was still going on about wedding dates and seating assignments. I barely heard him say he was leaving a lot of it up to Lashawn since he didn't really care.

"I'm good, nigga."

"Nah, he's coming to grips that his chick ain't really who he thought she was," Micah said.

Uriel looked confused at the random comment that Micah made, though it wasn't really random. For whatever reason, he was hating on Kiara, but I knew it was because she was Shaunte's best friend. Still, I wasn't even sure if he was right in his deduction or not. The truth was I hadn't even spoken to my girl since shooting her that text. She did try to call me, but I hadn't been keen to answer her. It'd been a few weeks since we spoke at all. So, I couldn't confirm or deny.

Uriel looked from me to Micah and started to laugh dryly.

"So, all that shit went in one ear and out the other, John? You really letting this nigga get into your head?"

"Don't act like I'm playing mind games when the proof is in the pudding. She cheated with you, so you don't think she'll cheat with him?"

"Let me holla at him," Uriel said. "I'll catch y'all later."

Micah looked shocked that Uriel even made the announcement. I knew if there'd been a polite way to kick Micah out without tossing out Xander he would've done it. But as it stood, the only other option was just to say he wanted to talk to me alone.

Xander stood up, motioning for Micah to follow suit. Micah shrugged, more laughter coming from him. They both dapped up Uriel. I accepted dap from Xander but looked at Micah's hand when he waited to do the same. I shook my head at him, still disappointed in the antics.

Even if Kiara was wrong, I didn't get how he got to stand on the side and speak on her name. We'd only ended up in this position because he showed up unceremoniously to my house.

"I mean, feel how you feel, Barnes. Still, don't make me wrong. Most of these chicks ain't worth a damn. Uriel got lucky."

Then he walked out the door. Xander sighed and followed after him and closed the door. Uriel sighed, running a hand down his face.

"Johnathan, what's going on?"

I sighed and then regaled him with what happened a few weeks ago. Uriel hummed, running a hand down his face.

"I mean, I know it looks bad but you're dragging it at this point, bro," Uriel said. "You don't know the context. You're just going off of the small moment you saw her laughing with him. How do you know she wasn't laughing at him?"

I thought about that, letting the thought marinate and had to nod at the other thought process I hadn't even considered. I just thought it was whack that she was sitting with him in the first place. What did they have to discuss?

"A whole court case," Uriel said, shrugging. "Maybe trying to slide his way back in so he doesn't have to sell the house. Another moment to try to rain on your parade like he's been doing this whole time. Julien's a narcissist. It used to always be about him, good or bad. Now it's about you and he doesn't like losing. Fuck the fact that he's moving on. You have to stop living in your emotions when it comes to yours. Yeah, love her but take inventory. Kiara's not who Micah says she is. She's who you know her to be. That's it, that's all."

I was stunned into silence by the way Uriel deduced the whole situation. It gave me perfect clarity. Again, I ran a hand down my face.

"It's coming up on that time when somebody's going to have to sit Micah down and say a few things to him. I don't know if it should be me or not. But in all honesty, I don't give a fuck if Kiara cheated on you, don't let him keep disrespecting your woman in your face like that, fam. If he had opened his mouth to say something crazy about Lashawn, it was coming down to blows. I know you don't want to disrespect because that's the homie but how much longer can the homie disrespect? John, get your shit together. Y'all niggas marching down the aisle together for my fuckin' wedding and I'm not trying to hear no goofy shit."

"Might need to switch up your list, homie," I sighed. "I don't even know if shorty gonna talk to me or not. It's been a few weeks."

"That's on you, nigga. I been told you to get right," Uriel tossed back. "Still, we're having an engagement party on Saturday. Get dressed up and get your woman back."

I opened my mouth to counter Uriel and was met with a hard glare.

"She was never your sis, to be honest, Barnes. She was always mine. So, I'm looking out for my sis at this point. Get your stupid ass dressed like you want your woman and get her back. You're looking miserable still trying to hold onto your pride. I'm not doing a second round of These Hoes Ain't Loyal."

I laughed and then gave my man dap as he chuckled as well.

"That's what I'm talking about. Get right, nigga."

Chapter Eleven

Kiara David

"I don't give a fuck that it's your wedding, sis. I'm not talking to him."

Lashawn cackled as we both got ready for her engagement party. I was envious of her glow. I wasn't even sure what got into Uriel after their whole breakdown but my friend stepped up with a ring and I had to admit a certain kind of envy that he understood how things worked in a relationship. I broke down and all I'd gotten from Johnathan was a dry text about what he didn't deserve and radio silence for about a month.

I wasn't even sure we were together anymore.

"No, because you didn't just call me the other day crying about it, right?" Lashawn asked. " You even called Shaunte about it?"

Shaunte had been dating Aldis for a few months now and based on everything she'd told us thus far; Micah was the last thing on her mind. The twosome were now engaged to be married and it taught me quite a bit outside of my own relationship that a man plays no games when he wants what he wants. Things were slow going for me and Johnathan based on me wanting to find healing after my relationship with Julien. While I wasn't totally upset with Johnathan, I was saddened that it'd been sometime since we spoke.

Still, that wasn't on me.

I hadn't bothered telling Shaunte about the fracas that had been going on mostly because I didn't want to bring Micah's name in her stratosphere. She was totally happy with her situation and though I wanted to lean on my friend for support and advice, I didn't think it wise to trouble her about Micah and Johnathan acting a fool.

Lashawn however, didn't give a good damn as she dialed up Shaunte and put her on speaker.

"Sis! Let me tell you what the fuck is going on..."

"Shawn! Stop it!" I yelled, reaching to end the phone call.

"Tell me what?" Shaunte said. "It's been kind of dry with no drama going on. I hate to brag but I haven't been pressed over shit lately."

"That's why I'm telling Shawn to hang up. She's being messy."

"No, ya girl is being stupid and needs someone to talk sense into her. Because her and Johnathan are not carrying on like this. Everybody better be happy and smiling on my wedding day or there'll be hell to pay."

Shaunte demanded to be put on FaceTime and I smiled upon seeing my beautiful friend's face. She smiled upon seeing mine, but her face hardened as she took a good look into my eyes.

"What's wrong with you, Key?"

"Micah's stupid ass."

Shaunte rose a perfectly arched brow and shook her head with light laughter escaping her lips.

"I know y'all not letting Micah shit all over y'all garden, sis. I just know it."

"Sis...it's gotten bad since he found out you got engaged."

"Hmph. So, none of these grown ass men telling this nigga to behave, huh?"

"Nope."

The 'p' sound was dramatic when I answered but this whole thing was dramatic. Still, I regaled her with the story and everything that happened between me and Johnathan from that day forward. I saw the sadness come into her eyes when she saw my eyes tearing up.

"It's obvious you miss him, Key. Honestly, it was a misunderstanding and I can't see why y'all can't talk that out."

"I think Micah has been in his ear so it's taking longer than it should," Lashawn said, shrugging. "Uriel been over here trying to keep his peace about it because he feels like John needs to regulate that."

"I mean, only thing she can do is show up at this party looking like a bag. I can only advise that you give him a hard time for being away but don't make shit harder on yourself, sis. He's missing you. You're missing him. Things shouldn't have gotten this out of hand. As for Micah...I might have to go ahead and talk to him."

"For what?" Lashawn said. "Listen sis, my thing is. We knew when you announced that Aldis was handling his business you weren't going back to Mike. His boys knew you weren't going back to Mike when he decided to be on playtime instead of grown man hour. Only person still thinking you coming back is Mike. That's on Mike. It's not on you. It's not on Kiara. It's not even on Johnathan or his boys to wipe his tears away. Niggas don't give a fuck about none of this shit he talking. They just don't want to upset him. But fuck all 'a' dat."

"I just want him to give my sis an apology because smearing her name is giving bitch vibes," Shaunte said. "I don't appreciate it at all. We all came up together and just because me and him don't rock together on that level anymore doesn't give him the right to make Key a target. I'll be damned."

"That's still for Johnathan to do," Lashawn said. "It's on us to show up at my party, look like a million bucks and celebrate this upcoming wedding that I ain't think I was getting. We gonna have a good time, Key and John gonna make up, and we all gonna welcome Aldis into the family. Mike gonna get with it or get lost. I don't give a fuck either way."

I shrugged because I felt the same way. I wasn't sure when me and Johnathan were going to make up, but I was taking my friend's advice and not being easy on him. I had no plans on doing anything but serving him the silence he served me when I tried to make things right, even though I had done no wrong.

The setting would be at Keen's Steakhouse and the party was basically to celebrate the upcoming nuptials and get the wedding party introduced to each other. Lashawn and Uriel weren't accepting Johnathan and I marching down their aisle with anyone else other than each other so they had double interest in us making up.

Maybe being alone with my ex in a Starbucks wasn't the best idea but he'd only gotten a solid three minutes. Johnathan missed the part where I gave Julien my ass to kiss and an impolite exit.

I wasn't prepared to face my "man", but I would. I just wasn't falling at his feet with an apology.

The ball was still in his court and the clock was ticking.

Johnathan Barnes

I rolled my eyes inwardly, unsure of why this was a whole black-tie event. Still, I decided on classic black and white since it wouldn't miss and pulled up. I was already humbled by Uriel days ago by his thought process on the mess I'd made of things. I wasn't even sure how, if at all, I would approach my lady...if she were still my lady at the end of the day. My text and subsequent radio silence might've given her the wrong idea and that would've again been my fault.

It hadn't taken long to get settled in. Walking up to the host's podium and having my name checked off the list got me a quick escort to the room where we'd be partying for the night. I was kind of impressed by the pomp and circumstance of the event and suddenly understood why Uriel had required the wait time for Lashawn. He wanted everything to be fit for the celebrations. Somehow, wanting everything to be top tier costs money. It was kind of rocky for them, but I was glad they came to an agreement and that the financial situation was enough to bring about moments such as these.

There'd been a long, communal table that would fit us all together. I cringed, seeing all the names outlined together. I was surprised to see Micah was showing up with a guest but decided not to dwell on that much. A few faces were already there including the guests of honor who sat near the end of the table. I was Uriel's best man, so my seat was next to him. Kiara's seat was vacated but she would sit across from me. I felt my stomach drop and felt the set up. I wanted to demand Uriel step outside so we could shoot the fair one. Still, I settled in, wondering why she was running late anyway.

Xander showed up with Tasha and she sat across from Xander who was seated next to me. Micah was the second to last one at the end with his "guest" seated across from him but next to Tasha. Shaunte was seated across from Aldis, her fiancé. Aldis was next to Micah, and I again wondered about the seating.

Xander took inventory himself and motioned for Micah to change seats with him. Their ladies took the hint and did the same. Micah's guest was the only one who'd been lost in the sauce as to what was going on, but she was polite about things and made the switch. I felt kind of bad that he would invite her knowing she wouldn't know anybody. I was grateful for Xander at that moment.

All gratefulness had walked out of the window when Kiara had stepped in. Her eyes were bright. Her makeup was gorgeous, and the dress reminded me of her birthday night mostly because it was a royal blue. It fit her curvy body as she sauntered to her assigned seat and sat across from me. I watched her eyes grow nervous as she laid them on me for the first time in weeks. I smirked, causing her to smirk back. Neither of us spoke but the energy was there.

I was grateful to be sitting down because had I been standing, I would've grown weak in the knees. As it were, laying eyes on her again caused me to rise in my pants and I cursed inwardly, not expecting to be as excited as I was.

I stared at her unabashedly, taking note of her hair being swept back into a semi-messy French roll and her silver and diamond jewelry making her look like the bag that I needed to walk out with. She talked with everybody around me but had yet to say two words to me.

Conversation was lively amongst almost everybody. Really only Micah was silent and testy. Shaunte and Aldis were somewhat in their own world, and I felt bad for my guy. Their attraction was palpable. Shaunte hadn't just been talking about moving on but actually had. Micah's guest was a lovely girl, but I could tell she was confused about why he was acting aloof. She did her best to entertain conversation with everyone else near her. Xander and Tasha had been a great help with that much.

Uriel and Lashawn were busy running their engagement story over and over to notice anybody else's discomfort in the room. I had to admit though, Lashawn was stunning. Her red floor length mermaid gown fit her like a glove. She was the personification of glowing and it was a reminder of the way she dropped into our lives almost overnight after Chantel became a thing of the past. My heart warmed looking at them as they gushed and still hoped it would be Kiara and I in the future.

That thought turned me to her, still laughing and carrying on with Lashawn. Our food came out in courses. Although I enjoyed the offerings I couldn't fully enjoy myself because I was too caught up in Kiara's every move. Uriel's words rang in my mind again, causing me to be abased at how I'd handled things. Uriel kept me occupied as much as he could have but it hadn't mattered. Past noticing other little details about the night, I couldn't keep my eyes off of Kiara. I was wondering how to get her alone without disrupting the entire party.

Music started to play and it was the cue for us to get up and start dancing. Still, I hesitated, wondering which way Kiara was going to go. I sighed as she pulled back her chair, making an excuse about heading to the bathroom. I waited a beat before following behind her. I took my time even as I watched her saunter towards the restroom. Then I called her name right when she reached for the door.

"What do you want, Johnathan?"

Her tone hadn't been sharp, but she was nervous.

"I want to talk, Key."

She was quiet and I saw the rise and fall of her shoulders before she turned to face me. I was shocked at the glitter of tears in her eyes.

"It's been weeks and now you want to talk? Talk about what, Johnathan? What is there left to talk about?"

"That I was wrong. I came to tell you that I was wrong and I'm sorry. I'm sorry, baby."

I walked up to her, in the narrow space, trapping her between me and the bathroom door. I stopped short, fighting against the urge to pull her into my arms and kiss her all over.

"Last time you said anything to me, you mentioned that you deserved better. You said that from making an assumption when I deserved better than you prioritizing your bitter ass friend over me."

"You're right, baby. Please understand me, I didn't mean to hurt your feelings. I just wanted to be there for my boy, but I know the way I went about it hurt you. I wasn't looking to hurt your feelings, but I thought I was protecting you."

"Protecting me would've been to tell me to wait for you in your room. I wasn't even totally mad at where your heart was, it was just how you did it. And then you ice me out for weeks because you think I'm low enough to run back to my ex-boyfriend?"

I opened my mouth when Kiara lifted her hand. I quieted immediately.

"Johnathan, I love you. I loved you while I was with him. I love you now but...that shit hurt me. I know you think we're still friends that have bomb sex sometimes but no, this isn't friends with benefits type shit."

She'd been pressing her finger into my chest while expressing herself. Her brows were furrowed.

"I get that now, baby."

I took her hand in mine as she pulled away. She flinched slightly but didn't pull away from me. Small hope bloomed into my chest as I caressed the top of her hand. She looked up at me, still blinking away her tears.

"Do you? Because I can't go through you icing me out and thinking you can keep coming back in. I'm not with those games anymore. I've learned what it means to love me and to put myself first and make no mistake, I love you more than any man I've been with, but I will leave."

She pulled her hand away and then folded her arms. I knew she did it to reinforce her point and it had the intended effect of making my heart ache at the loss of contact. She was driving her point home and it forced me to sigh, humbling myself further to get back into her good graces.

"Yes, I get it. I thought I understood but it took all that for me to understand...you're my woman and that's across the board. I won't do that to you, ever again."

I reached out for her, caressing her face with my hand. I was surprised that she allowed me to touch her. I was even more surprised when she leaned into my touch.

"Forgive me, baby," I said. "What I gotta do to make it up to you?"

I moved fully into her space, pulling her into my arms. I felt her melt against me, and I let go of a sigh. Lifting her face up by her chin I told her she looked beautiful. I enjoyed the blush that filled her cheeks when I said so and leaned in, taking a chaste kiss from her lips.

"Take me home," she said, grinning. "I don't want to keep standing next to this bathroom door."

"You left anything in the dining room?" I questioned.

"Yeah, I need my bag."

We walked quietly back, hand-in-hand. I stroked the top of her hand, reveling in the fact that I was holding my love's hand again. I looked down at her, feeling my heart burst at the fact that she allowed me to be by her side again.

We walked back in, earning different glances from different people. I ignored the fake disgust I read in Micah's eyes while he danced with a woman he hadn't even bothered to introduce to any of us.

"I see we're all just gluttons for punishment," Micah said, chuckling. "Don't say I didn't try to warn you."

Kiara had stopped short of meeting me halfway when Micah made the remark. His smirk made me close my fists and caused me to step in front of my woman to face him. The smirk he wore dropped from his face and I was saddened, mostly because the woman with him was still lost on what was going on.

"I think you need to get your shit together, Mike. I tried to keep it calm because I know you're going through some things but this right here?"

I motioned to Kiara, taking her hand in mine and pulling her in closer.

"I made it a fact years ago that I didn't play about her. That was common knowledge beforehand and it means double now. I didn't want to bring that heat to you because you're my boy, but you keep at it you gonna see me."

"You dead ass, nigga? We've been friends for years and this how you moving?"

"Yeah, nigga. Not once did I disrespect you, ever. I tried to show you grace but now you're taking me for a fucking pussy and I'm not gonna keep doing it. I suggest you walk light when it comes to her and find a better way to wipe your tears, nigga. This ain't it."

Micah opened his mouth then closed it. Words eluded him, even as my features hardened. I was ashamed that I had to come down on him at this moment, but he wouldn't stop unless I made him do so. I'd apologize to Uriel and Lashawn later.

I walked away, Kiara still in tow. Before we walked out of the door, I motioned for her to walk in front of me. I lightly pushed her lower back to guide her outside of the dining room. Once we made it out into the street, I pulled my woman in closer to me, totally understanding her anger.

I had been too focused on Micah's pain to have regard for hers the way I should have. Now that my mind was clearer, more shame came down on me for how I was moving. I was left confused on why he was making Kiara a target, anyway. His problem was with Shaunte, so he needed to keep it with Shaunte.

"Baby, forgive me."

I lifted her face once more to look into her eyes. I had meant it earlier, but I doubly meant it then. It'd been one thing when he was drunk. Now he kept soberly stating his distaste and it angered me. My woman was as honorable as they came and even if she weren't, nobody had a place to speak badly on her. It was something that would never happen again.

Kiara sighed. "I forgive you, Johnny."

"I'll make it up to you, baby. I promise."

Kiara grabbed my hand. Reaching up, she caressed my face with a smile.

"You already did," She said. "Let's go home."

Home had turned out to be my house. Time hadn't been wasted once we'd gotten out of the Uber and past the threshold. Her hands were tangled in my shirt. Suit jacket and shirt joined each other piled up on the floor while I messed up her makeup with kisses all over her face. I fumbled with her zipper as she fumbled with my belt. Moans and groans intermingled as we took kisses from each other, making up for lost time. My hand was up her dress, reacquainting myself with her love and groaning at how wet she was for me. I decided not to make her wait, finding her spot and bringing her to completion.

My entire name dragged out of her mouth as a groan, and I snatched the breath out of her with the next kiss. I wasn't even sure how my pants finally dropped but when they did, Kiara grabbed me, making me grit my teeth at how she pulled me into full hardness.

"Wait, baby, wait," she moaned, turning around. "The zipper's there."

She pointed at it and my trembling fingers pulled it down, allowing her to step out of the dress. I hadn't wasted another moment afterward, pushing her down onto my couch and climbing on top of her. A second hadn't passed before I was inside of her again, driving her into another orgasm. Tears left her eyes as I kept pressing, cursing the good feelings as I pulled her arms above her head and pushed her off the precipice again.

I leaned in, kissing along her chest and pulling a nipple into my mouth. I slowed down, taking the moment to enjoy her.

"It's been too long, baby."

A quick slap hit my face and my eyes widened to see Kiara looking at me with a look of reproof. I chuckled, leaning in to kiss her lips, sliding her my tongue.

"Whose fault was that?"

"I know, baby. I know."

I reached under, making sure to notch her clit just so when I thrust the pleasure would run through her. I was rewarded with her moans and mewls as I'd done so.

"I'm gonna spend all night making it right."

For the rest of the night, that was my mission.

Chapter Twelve

Kiara David

I sighed, lavishing in all the attention Johnathan was giving me. He'd been laying sweet kisses all over my face since we finally found our way to his bed. I was lying between his legs, with my back against his chest. He held me around my waist, my hands in his while he whispered his apologies. Although I told him I'd forgiven him, he was still apologetic.

"You looked so beautiful earlier, that shit hurt," he said. "Should've been walking in with me but that's on me, baby."

I wanted to stop him from apologizing and spewing his regrets. I knew I wouldn't hold on to my anger much longer when I got everything off my chest at the restaurant. I'd already forgiven him when I looked into his face and fell all over myself when he'd grinned at me. Still, I knew I couldn't let it all go until I aired him out.

"Johnny," I said. "Baby..."

"I love you, Key," he said, sighing. "I...don't want you to ever have to question it. I don't want you to ever have to wonder at all. I love you. I don't play cool about you. I haven't done that stupid shit since high school. I love you and I want you. Nothing or no one is going to make you have to question that again."

He said it with such finality that I was speechless. I knew most of that had to do with Micah's foolishness for the past few weeks. I knew that it was hard for him to talk to his friend harshly and put him in check. At least those were my thoughts about it.

I had an inkling that our relationship would change quite a few of the relationships we had with other people, but I hadn't once thought Micah turning on us would be an effect of it. I hoped that they made up but the way I was set up, I never had to talk to him ever again. To question my integrity on a regular basis was crazy. To bully me was crazy. To basically use me as a whipping boy was crazy. I knew in my heart he was never coming to Shaunte with the same energy. It was a shame he wanted to try it with me.

"I love you, Johnny. And I don't wonder at all if you love me. My wonder is if you trust me."

I shifted so that I could straddle him and look into his eyes. They were cast downward, and I knew the shame had hit as I bought back up the text message he sent me. I laid my hand on his cheek and caressed him gently.

"I remember when you used to keep me company after Julien would leave me hanging for days on end. He wouldn't come back around until word got around that we were hanging out. Suddenly, he had to remind me that I had a man. But we both knew what it was."

Johnathan chuckled. "Yeah. I was always waiting for you to say something, but you never would."

"I wanted to! Believe me, I did. But I was with Julien. In my mind, I never forgot he was my man, even as badly as he was treating me. Being around you was always so good. You were my best friend in the world...and the man I loved the most. Still, I had to be loyal to Julien. At least as loyal as I could be."

Johnathan chuckled. "I get it, baby."

"Hm. I don't think you do. What I'm saying is he treated me badly and I rode it out with him. So how could I betray you and you treat me so well?"

Johnathan was silent as he leaned into my touch. He made a vulnerable, yet beautiful picture. It was enough for me to lean in and kiss him softly on the lips. I pulled back, smirking at him.

"It's not just something to say when I say it's always been you," I said. "It's always been you. I just never thought I could be with you. So now I am and there's nothing in the world I would ever do to mess that up."

Johnathan nodded.

"The optics were bad, baby. I get that part. I just wished you would have questioned me on it instead of assuming. I'm your woman and I couldn't have been mad had you asked me what the fuck was going on?"

"I mean, baby. I still felt like I deserved better," he shrugged. "And you're right. You are my woman...that looked real bad with you in there, fucking guffawing. And yeah, I should've asked you. But yeah, I was afraid. We already had beef and I didn't know just how hard you took it. I didn't think it was that bad until I saw you in there with him and then wondered if I missed anything? I admit that I was fearful of losing you over a mishap."

"Well, let me explain," I giggled. "Julien basically tried to sweet talk me out of my money from the house. He saw a post Mike made and decided to take that as an in. He pretty much asked if you and I were over and said if I asked him nicely, I could move back in with him."

Johnathan's frowned, seeing exactly what I saw in that moment, slowly started to laugh. His chuckles built until it was full blown laughter. Tears rolled down his face at the absurdity and the audacity.

"In another scenario, I might've pulled up to this nigga's house and punched him in the mouth."

"There's no need for all of that," I rolled my eyes.

"You're right," he said. "Still. The audacity is enough of a reason."

"Yeah. You saw me at the wrong time," I said, sighing. "So, I get it."

"Hm. Yeah if I knew that was the conversation, I wouldn't have done all that."

"Well, I say all that to say, you can trust me, baby. I'm not like that."

"I knew better. I had a moment."

"No more moments."

I flicked his nose, giggling as he sucked his teeth and then started to tickle me. He tickled me until I cried for surrender. He smirked triumphantly, while I caught my breath.

"I win."

"You win biggest nose of the year," I said, shrugging. "Now I'm out of energy, I'm going to bed."

"I can't tickle you anywhere else?"

I giggled as he reached between my legs and started to massage me again. I moaned lightly, attempting to bat his hand away.

"No, Johnny! I'm tired!"

"Tired? You weren't tired when you flicked at my nose," he said, "Now I wanna bury it in something."

"Mm-mm," I shook my head. "I'm ready to go to bed. Get some in the morning."

"Wore that out, huh? I guess I can accept defeat."

Johnathan pulled his hand away and instead pulled back the covers. I smiled as he motioned for me to join him and did, laying my body on top of his, with my head on his chest. I sighed slowly as he kissed my forehead.

"I love you, Johnny."

"I love you more, Key."

I sighed deeply, leaning up to kiss his chin and being grateful for the peace that settled after our fall out. We had work to do as a couple overall, but I had hope that this time around things would work out. On that last thought, sleep took over my body and I slept soundly.

Johnathan Barnes

Xander and I shot the shit for a few hours. We sat out on my front porch, drinking a beer and sharing old war stories. It was the next evening and all was right in my soul. Kiara was in my kitchen, making something for us to eat. The thought of her cursing to herself while she made dinner perfect moved me in a way I could barely explain. I just knew all was right with the world like my woman was home. Of course, she wasn't calling it home altogether yet, but I knew the time was drawing near.

"Gave Mike the old heave-ho and then left with your woman. I ain't mad at you, Barnes."

I busted out laughing, taking another sip of my beer. Xander clinked his beer can with mine, chuckling.

"Ain't last two hours. Gave it a calm, oh, I'm gonna show my face."

I shook my head. "Aye, listen. I felt bad. I didn't mean to leave so abruptly but she was feeling it and I was feeling it. I wished I could've spoken to Mike in private."

"You always been a classy nigga, but you had to publicly come at him," Xander shrugged, taking a sip of his own. "He didn't give a fuck about your feelings or her feelings in none of it. Plus, he was starting to get too comfortable. I was about ready to pull him to the side because he's forgetting that's still sis at the end of the day. I don't give a fuck if you fucking her or not."

"That's what I didn't understand. She won't be hanging out with us the same way and all because I'm tagging that but-"

"-look at you. Being a nigga about it and shit," Xander cut me off, chuckling. "Yeah, I'm clappin' that now, nigga. Check me out."

I snickered and shrugged my shoulders. "I'm not ashamed of it. I'm ashamed that I waited so long but I'm not ashamed of it."

"You're not supposed to be. I'm just laughing at your ass. I ain't gonna front. I thought the whole birthday party idea was stupid until I sat back and realized...this nigga never really did anything on that level for her. Apart from the house, I couldn't really see what he was good for."

"Y'all were cool, though."

"He was aight. You know I would've held you down though if you wanted to pull up on the nigga. I wasn't going out like you ain't my boy. You know I'm solid."

If nothing else, crazy as Xander could be, he was a solid friend. That much I could give him.

"My bad though, I cut you off," he chuckled. "What bothered you?"

"Nah, overall, we were all friends. Why Mike coming at mine like she a city girl?"

Xander was silent for a minute and looked me in the eye. I looked back, thinking he was going to say something profound. He took a long sip of his beer and then looked back out into the street.

"Because...he's a bitch."

He said the sentence so calmly I thought he'd hit me with the ways of the universe. When I realized it was the opposite, my laughter couldn't be contained and I cursed at my friend, who laughed back in response, shrugging his shoulders helplessly.

"What? You thought I had a real answer? I ain't have an answer for that shit. I've been embarrassed for weeks over this shit because I can't understand it. It's like I said, you had to come at him for real, in front of everybody so he could understand what he was doing was fuck shit. I'm glad L talked to you because he was raring to go on that same campaign over me and Tasha. I wasn't going to be polite at all."

I was silent on that note, taking another swig.

"The thing is, he wants somebody to blame. He doesn't want to blame himself because he feels like Shaunte woke up overnight and felt the way she did. I thought so too at first, that's why I was like nah, fuck all that, get right. But I got to see him firsthand. Mike wasn't ready to settle, and he was curious about new pussy. He thought he was going to Donnell Jones his way around and then come back but that swee-lil-dee-doop-dee-dee shit wasn't working for sis."

I chuckled. "Nigga."

"Nah. Break down the song and that right there was essentially Mike. He just forgot to put it out there for her but thought that she'd be silently waiting in the corner for him to get right and then come back home. But you can't have your cake and eat it. That's why I never fathomed wifing a chick at the stage I was at. It wasn't fair. I was more like DMX in What These Bitches Want."

"I gave you what you gave me, boo," I quoted, shrugging my shoulders. "Nah, you got a point. Sounds like you did know."

"Lowkey," he chuckled. "I mean, he's heartbroken. That part isn't hard to figure out. The whole bullying Kiara part was wild. I was waiting for you to say something. I think you had to realize we couldn't handle shit the normal way no more."

"Yeah, I did. It didn't hit me that...I'm tagging that for real. I was still in a daze. I don't even think Mike realized it entirely until I said something. Shit was childish as fuck the way he kept coming. I guess he thought she was going to just snuff him one time and then be done with it and it's like nah. Niggas are grown now. We handle shit differently. We're not going down this road no more. That's my dude but...nah. The moment he decides he wants to move onto something else and it gets serious, there's no room for me to be talking shit about that woman. So, he's not doing it to mine."

"I thought I was gonna have to learn you, G," he said, chuckling. "I know you kept it G for L and Shawn but... should've snuffed him."

I chuckled, shaking my head. "Nah. That was their moment and I ain't want to soil it by punching this nigga in the mouth. Plus, we wouldn't have been cool at all after that. I wasn't going to fight fair."

Which would have caused a breakdown in our friendship. Then he would've expected people to take sides. In his state of mind, he would've ended up either distancing himself or we would have distanced ourselves. It wasn't going to go well either way.

"How are you feeling, though? How's Tash treating you?"

"Changed a nigga life in one night. I was stuck then and I'm still stuck. I ain't even tried getting out."

Xander laughed lightly, looking down into his beer, a faraway look on his face. He shook it off, sipping on the beer to finish it off and smiled.

"That's bae. That's pretty much all I can say. Got a whole block list behind her. She got me explaining to my old hoes that I'm good. They still confused. Shit, I'm still confused but...she's it and that's all."

"You talked crazy about ole girl, now look."

Xander shrugged. "She made her point with her petty ass and now she's stuck, too. So, we stuck. Give it a year and some change a nigga might be proposing."

My face read shock after the announcement. If we were different men, I would've laid a hand on top of Xander's forehead to make sure he was feeling well. As it were, Xander tossed a cuss word at me that made me chuckle.

"I know, I know. I mean, she changed my mind. I thought nobody was worth it but...she showed me different. I'll lay a nigga to rest over that. I don't have any complaints. She trusts me. She got her own shit going on and she does her thing. There's no reason for me not to move forward with her. I ain't gonna lie though, Shaun checked my temperature when she saw me. I said the same thing to her."

Again, laughter fell over me. I mentioned that that had been my exact thoughts when he said what he told me. It was drastically different from last year before he ran into Latasha. I thought he was never settling down.

Ever.

"I'm happy for you. Proud of you, even."

"I'm almost proud of you, too, Johnny-Boy. Next time though, knock that nigga out."

"Stop tempting my man to do foolish shit and y'all come on in and eat."

We both looked up to see Kiara's head poking out of the front door. I smiled dopily as I saw her face.

"I'm about to grab mine to go, sis," Xander announced. "I'm about to pop up on my girl and get on her nerves."

"Don't go over there stressing my friend out. But if you're about to leave, make her a to-go, too."

I followed behind her as she walked in. I popped her backside just because and she turned around, fixing me with a withering look that didn't reach her eyes. I smirked, walking to see what the spread was and grinned.

This time it was spaghetti. I grinned at the wine that she had in a glass decanter and smirked as she proudly stated the ingredients. I learned that she used some ground sirloin, Italian sausage, and filet mignon in what she called grown folks' spaghetti; a recipe adapted from YouTuber, stovetopkisses. Xander chuckled as he fixed his plate and one for his love and laughed at the jokes she made about not being ready for what was in store.

"I can't wait. I been wanting to make that recipe for weeks," Kiara stated. "I know it's gonna hit even more tomorrow."

Which was the best part about pasta dishes. I was glad she made a sizable amount since I'd be out and about with showings the next morning. For the moment however, I was going to enjoy my woman and my night.

I walked my friend out the door after he thanked Kiara for her hospitality and joked about her growing up.

"Rough and tumble becoming Chef Boyardee protégé and shit. Love that for you, sis."

In only the way he could, he made Kiara laugh even while she cursed him out. He chuckled, pulling her into a one-armed hug. It was a stark contrast to the way Micah had been treating her as of late and made me wonder if they'd ever get back to that stage. Could the camaraderie even be restored? Was Kiara even missing it overall?

I decided if we got back, cool. If we didn't, then we didn't. I hoped for the former but knew I wouldn't be broken up over the latter.

"I'm out. I'll let you know when I made it."

I chuckled. "Say that."

My friend then made his way, and I turned my attention back to my love.

Kiara was setting up the table for us and I hung back, watching her. I licked my lips in appreciation. She looked so comfortable in my space as always. I pictured her suddenly, yelling at our children to wash their hands and get ready to eat. I pictured myself, wrapping my arms around her waist and laying a fat one on her cheek in gratitude to her labor. I could almost hear our children crying for us to calm down with the display, but we'd ignore them. I'd slap her ample backside for good measure and-

"Johnny."

I blinked out of my trance and smiled, embarrassed at how I had to look.

"Yeah, baby?"

"I was calling you. You not hungry?"

"I am. I was stuck just looking at you."

Kiara blushed, biting her lip. "Don't start."

"Don't start what? I'm just explaining why I ain't hear nothing for about thirty seconds."

I reached for her face, caressing her cheek. I leaned in, taking a quick kiss from her lips. I pulled away, walking over to the table.

We enjoyed our meal together. I was grateful for the synergy between myself and my love. I had paused her when she began picking up our dishes and told her I'd take care of it. She put away the food we hadn't eaten however and then disappeared.

Once I had finished, I decided to look for her. I heard the water running from my bathroom the closer I'd gotten to my room. I smiled as I saw my love preparing a bath.

"Hm. You spoiling me tonight, huh?" I questioned. "Or is this for you?"

"It's for us," She smiled. "Regular shit."

I laughed, remembering the first time I'd said those words to her. I watched her again as she disrobed down to nothing and tossed her clothes in my hamper. I again noted the familiarity and wondered if it'd be too much for me to assume she was ready to move in. I swallowed the question that came unbidden in my mind, again leaving it up to her to decide when.

"You're not joining me, Johnny?"

Her voice was throaty. I wasn't sure she understood what happened to me when she used that tone with me.

I'd already been in the mood but now the ache was running up and through me. Nothing was going to cure the ache except her.

I disrobed, tossing my clothes to the side, and walked up to where she was at the side of the tub. I leaned in once more, kissing her lips. This time, I took my time, sliding my tongue into her mouth and groaning when she returned my affections. I reached to take a breast in my hand when she pulled back.

"Don't start."

"Now you're just torturing me, baby."

"I don't want the water to go cold."

I smirked and then settled in the tub, hard as a rock. Kiara lowered herself in after me, laying against my chest. I then decided to take a breast in my hand and rub a nipple. Her moan hadn't gone unnoticed by me.

"Oh, I can start now?" I questioned, kissing along her neck. "You ran out of excuses?"

She giggled. "Yes. I couldn't just stand for a nice, hot bath to go to waste. I even put towels in the warming rack."

"Hm. I think you still should've just let me get some," I said, "I would've made it up to you."

I reached in front of me, rubbing the small bundle that made her quake for me every time. A hiss left her mouth as I'd done so.

"I have to admit to you looking so right in my house," I said, still rubbing her. "You sure you're not ready to be here for real, baby?"

I cursed myself in my mind for asking the question. Still, I'd already asked, and I'd just take whatever answer she gave me.

"Hm. I've been thinking about it," she said. "It feels like home to me now."

I lazily played with her, enjoying the noises she made. Once she got too excited, I pulled back, letting her live in the same tension she was forcing me to live in.

"So, what's stopping you? Am I missing something?"

"I want to be your wife first."

I felt my heartbeat quicken.

"That's it? That's the only thing?"

I felt Kiara's nod and the sound of her agreement ending on another moan.

"If I knew that..."

Kiara giggled. "It's always that easy for you, huh?"

"Yes! I told you it was always that easy for me. I already said I'd show you that everything you missed with him you have with me. You thought it was a joke?"

"No, you just keep surprising me. That's all."

I paused my ministrations, pulling her into me with both of my arms. I started kissing along her shoulder.

"I've loved you since we were kids, Kiara. I always loved you. We kept saying we were friends, but we were always more. L said it the other day that honestly...we were never friends. I think circumstance made it that we started off that way, but we weren't going to ever stay friends. It just took longer than expected to make you mine. I loved you from the first time you socked me in the mouth and then bought me ice to stop the swelling."

She giggled at the memory.

"I loved you from the time you fought this girl who tried to bully me...you knew I didn't want to hit her, so you got her for me."

"I loved you for not wanting to hit her," she said. "I wanted to hit her for thinking she had a pussy on her hands."

I grinned, kissing her shoulder once more in reply.

"Our history is long. The wait was long. I want you here, baby. So, whatever I have to do to get you home, I'm going to do it. You think I don't want you here?"

"I know you do."

"So, stop being surprised. It took me a while to get to you, but all the red tape is out the way. You're mine and I've been wanting to marry you. I just knew I had to wait for you to be ready."

"So, you've been ready to have home cooked meals and me in an apron?"

"And nothing else."

"So fuckin' mannish."

"You fuck with it heavy so whatever."

She giggled, leaving my retort in the air. I only laughed in response, enjoying her body against mine.

Before long, we made our way to the shower. It was a slow episode of getting cleaned up. Mostly because of all the kissing that was being done. I was shocked when my woman grabbed me and pulled me back into full hardness. I'd been in a semi state the whole time, again waiting for the right moment.

"I told you that you could start," Kiara giggled. "Now you looking all shocked."

My chuckle was deep as I pushed her against the shower wall and pulled one of her legs up. I slid inside of her without hesitation and thrust until I reached her hilt. Her gasp let me know I'd gotten her back and the moan she let loose when I continued let me know all was forgiven. I melted as she wrapped her arms around my neck, pulling me into her lips.

"I love you, Johnathan Barnes."

"I love you, too, future Kiara Barnes."

She giggled but I saw her eyes melt and realized she liked the sound of it. I hadn't even bothered telling her that I liked the sound of it more. I was already planning a visit to the jewelry store in the back of my mind so she could pick out the style she wanted. Only thing she wouldn't see coming is the moment I was going to get on bended knee.

All that aside, I slowly and deeply loved on my woman until she climaxed. I made it a point to make her climax again and again. The moment was just for her to see how excited I was that she was ready to move forward. I knew we had things to work on but I'd rather she be around for us to work on them than in another space. Although I knew the time alone was crucial for us to move forward, I was also excited about our coming together.

I felt that familiar stir in my heart that I hadn't understood when I was a young boy and laid eyes on her. All I knew was that she was different from any other girl in the neighborhood. When she started to bloom into a woman that same stir didn't make sense. Not until Xander started making noises about approaching her. That burn had been so bright I was ready and willing to break his arm over it. That was until he started laughing at the fact that he saw me so clearly.

As a grown man, the stir was all so familiar, and I'd stopped running from the discomfort it gave me. I was in love and been in love with her before she could fathom the same love for me. Or maybe she already had fallen but by the time I'd done so, I was worse off. As they say the girl falls first but the boy falls worse.

Our moment in the shower ended with us preparing for bed. I lotioned her body down, taking in every detail that still excited me. I laid a kiss on her cheek when I finished and denied her when she told me to switch positions on our bed so she could return the favor.

"What you mean, no?"

"It means I'm going to handle myself. You relax."

Kiara rolled her eyes and sat up.

"This thing goes both ways."

I looked into her eyes and smirked at her pout. I handed her the lotion I wanted to apply on myself and laid down and relaxed as she started to rub me down.

"Thought so."

I swallowed a chuckle at her retort, knowing that'd be a whole fight if I let a chuckle slip. Still, I melted when she laid butterfly kisses on my cheek.

It'd taken quite a few years to reach this point and it almost seemed surreal. The love of my life in my arms and in my bed. Soon, she would be my wife. It was all real, a reality I couldn't have dreamed up better myself. She was love in motion and I would cherish her always.

www.ingramcontent.com/pod-product-compliance
Lightning Source LLC
LaVergne TN
LVHW090515110826
845146LV00003B/864

* 9 7 9 8 9 8 5 2 0 6 0 5 0 *